I0609615

William Wetmore Story

Vallombrosa

William Wetmore Story

Vallombrosa

ISBN/EAN: 9783337142544

Printed in Europe, USA, Canada, Australia, Japan

Cover: Foto ©Andreas Hilbeck / pixelio.de

More available books at **www.hansebooks.com**

VALLOMBROSA

BY

W. W. STORY

AUTHOR OF 'ROBA DI ROMA,' 'GRAFFITI D'ITALIA,'
'NERO,' ETC. ,

WILLIAM BLACKWOOD AND SONS
EDINBURGH AND LONDON
MDCCCLXXXI

GIFT

VALLOMBROSA.

IN the latter part of last October I found myself
in the lower slopes of the Apennines, on the
shadowy hills of Vallombrosa. Its very name,
which Milton has made familiar to English ears,
has a poetic and romantic attraction ; and when-
ever it is pronounced, there rises in the memory
his famous simile of the innumerable legions of
angelic forms

> " who lay entranced,
> Thick as autumnal leaves that strow the brooks
> In Vallombrosa, where the Etrurian shades
> High overarched embower."

But of the many who know by heart these
magical lines, how few there are to whom Vallom-

brosa is more than a sounding name—suggesting at best some vague place in the ideal realm of dreams, through whose dense Etrurian coverts of unnamed trees a fine poetic sunlight faintly shimmers, whose dim and shadowy paths and singing brooks are strewn by the ruffling winds of autumn with a wealth of innumerable leaves, and over which there hovers an undefined mysterious charm of unreality! Such at least it was to me before I visited it in the body. Nor did I find the dream those few lines had the power to evoke to my imagination, quite untrue to fact. Nothing could be more romantic, beautiful, and interesting in every way—whether sleeping and murmurous with whispers in the summer and autumn, with shadowy coverts for meditation, or rousing and wrestling with the storm-winds that descend upon it from the higher Apennines and assail its forests with their fury in the winter months. It is never tame or characterless, but silent, wild, lonely, secluded, gentle, or furious, according to the mood of the season, and responsive to every touch of feeling and passion.

I had been invited by a friend to pass a few days with her and her family in one of the most lonely regions of the large tract which bears the name of Vallombrosa. The once famous convent lies at a distance of about three miles from this spot; and here, in one of the hollows, they had hired an old deserted house, built centuries ago by the Medici as a stronghold and hunting-box, which they had fitted up and put into habitable condition as a summer retreat from the heats of Florence. Originally the house was flanked by two tall towers, and was castellated in form; but within the last few years the present Government, caring little for the picturesque, and apparently seeking rather to obliterate than to preserve the traces of the past, had ruthlessly and for no sufficient reason levelled the two towers and razed the upper storey : so that the house is now a square unpicturesque but solidly - built construction in stone, two storeys high, and with walls massive enough to resist the assault of anything but modern cannon. Here my friends had made their summer home, far from all society and neighbours, to enjoy freedom, solitude, and the silence and charm of nature. There is no highway to lead the wandering tourist to their doors, and only friends who are willing to brave a long romantic mountain-path practicable but to foot-passengers, or donkeys, or *treggie,* find their way to this solitary spot. These *treggie* are merely the rudest kind of sledge, made of two long solid planks, with a seat midway, which are trailed along the ground by patient slow-moving oxen. No carriage on wheels could possibly bear the shock and strain of these rough roads, if roads they can be called, which rather resemble the rock-strewn ways worn by mountain-torrents. So

one is not liable to morning calls in the latest
of Worth's dresses, God be thanked; but the
foot-passenger in stout boots and country dress
is amply repaid for his walk, whether he come
by the way of Podere Nuovo on the north, along
a winding path through the woods, or by the
monastery on the south, over a road commanding
the loveliest and largest views over an exquisite
and varied valley strewn with far-gleaming villages and towns, bounded by swelling outlines
of hills or mountains, one rising after another
against the delicate sky.

There, far away in the misty distance, can be
seen the vague towers and domes of Florence;
and through the valley the Arno and the Sieve
wind like silver bands of light, through olive-
covered slopes and vineyards that lie silent in
the blue haze of distance, spotted by wandering
cloud-shades, and taking every hue of changeful
light from the pearly gleams of early morning

to the gorgeous golden transmutations of twilight and the deep intensity of moonlit midnight.   Nearer, magnificent chestnuts throng the autumnal slopes, their yellow leaves glowing in the autumn sun.   Sombre groves of firs, marshalled along the hillsides for miles, stand solemn and dark.   Beech-trees rear at intervals their smooth trunks, or gather together in close and murmurous conclave.   The lower growth of gorse, and broom, and brush, and feathered fern roughen the hills, where the axe has bereft them of their forest-growth; and in every direction are wild enchanting walks through light and shadow, alluring us on and on for miles.   Here and there columns of wavering blue smoke tower and melt away into the blue sky, where the charcoal-burners are at work.   Little brooks come trickling down at intervals, finding their devious way among the rocks and leaves, and singing to themselves a low and silvery song. Now and then a partridge whirs up beneath

your feet, or a whistling woodcock suddenly
takes flight, or a startled hare with up-cocked
tail may be seen tilting through the underbrush,
or a sly fox steals cautiously away.

These foxes, which are very numerous, are the
bane of the place. They destroy the ground
game; and as it would not be possible to hunt
them with hounds over this wild and rugged
country, they are here merely a pest, and hateful
to sportsmen. Were it not for them and poach-
ers (who, indeed, are comparatively few), the
game ought to be most abundant; for the whole
country is Government property, fairly well
preserved by the forest-guards, and none but a
privileged few are permitted to shoot over it.

Small birds, however, of every kind abound,
and the woods are musical all the spring and
early summer with their happy song. Here at
Vallombrosa itself they are protected against
their bitterest enemy, man, and from the un-
sportsman-like devices of net and snare, which

are prevalent elsewhere throughout Italy.   But on the confines these are freely practised ; and the Government grants to a very limited extent, and for the small annual tax of fifteen francs, the right of snaring by means of the *paretaio*, as it is called.   This is a long, low, narrow erection, some six feet high in front, and covered with a roof sloping down to the ground behind.   The front is pierced with slits for outlook ; and within, the sportsmen, if they are to be honoured by such a name, hide themselves.   It is placed generally on open ground, with a square open space before it, so as to be exposed to the sight of all birds.   In this space a number of caged singing-birds are set at intervals, to attract by their song all other wandering birds.   On either side of this square extends flat along the ground a framed net, concealed often by brushwood and seeded plants, and connected with the inside of the *paretaio* with cords, by which they are worked.   Attracted by the murmur and flutter

of the caged **birds**, gradually all the **others in**
the **vicinity** gather about the place **and descend**
to the ground—curious, apparently, to investi-
gate the meaning of this strange **construction**,
and **to make** inquiries. **When a** sufficient
number **are** thus inveigled, **the cords are** suddenly **drawn, and** the **nets shut** instantly together
over the **space**, entrapping **the poor** unfortunates.
Sometimes **in one** of these *paretaii* **a** hundred
little **birds will** be taken **in a** day; and what-
ever they are, large or small, they **go to the spit**
or the pan, and find a place on the table.

Formerly, the snare and net were universal
in Italy, **and all** along the coast, in **the season**
of flight; **quails** were **thus** taken **by** tens **of**
thousands **as they** alighted weary with **their**
long flight from Africa. **But** of late the **present**
Government has strictly prohibited this practice,
and now they are only allowed to be shot in a
sportsmanlike manner. ˙ Still, **in the inland,**
netting and snaring are almost universal; **and**

everything is considered fair game, from the smallest sparrow to the pheasant and wild duck.

But at Vallombrosa, despite these snares, the woods are enlivened by the song of many a bird in summer: and now, in the mid-autumn, they still echo to the shrill scolding of the jay; the piping of the thrush, blackbird, and chaffinch; and the cheeping notes and trills of the lesser tribes. Squirrels swing from bough to bough, and run up the tall trunks. Grasshoppers flutter about, and, spreading their gay shards, show the gleam of blue wings beneath. And there is busy insect-life swarming, buzzing, and whispering everywhere in the woods. If one could only know what they are saying!

"To one who has been much in city pent" it is a pure delight, on bright autumnal days in late October, to wander through the woods and along the hillsides of Vallombrosa, vaguely, without object, dreaming, listening, at one with nature ; **now** climbing through the tangled gorse, **up** steep rugged declivities, **or** lingering **where** the roaring torrent dashes down **its** turbulent sheets of foam ; now following the track of some mountain **stream** through beech - groves ; now lying at rest **under** some **golden chestnut—** whose spiny burrs, showing the dark and polished **nuts within** their cloven husk, strew the rough grass underneath; now lingering to gaze **out** over **the** rolling distance below, so silent and lovely ; **now** treading the brown soft carpet beneath the tall columnal firs, whose serried masts rise thickly, climbing to the light, and swaying **to** the breeze, **and** whispering **to** it unimaginable secrets **beyond** our sense **to** catch.

On either side of **the** house are silent cathe- drals **of** firs, **into** which one can **enter** almost **with a step.** The summer sun pierces not through their summits ; **but all is cool and** shadowy, and filled with **a** sort **of dim religious**

light. Straighter pillars never were raised to
heaven, and finer murmurs of aspirations never
were heard in any human church. What do
they long for, these ever-whispering firs, that
are always remembering the murmur of the
distant sea ?

   This is the country in summer days, or in
the quiet days of sunny autumn ; but it has its
wilder days of passion and tempest, when the
gale sweeps down the clefts of the Apennines,
and wakes to stormy music the wondrous harp
of nature.   Then the whole forest roars in
answer to its call, and groans and quivers in its
every fibre, and rouses and wrestles with this
great invisible power, and shakes abroad its
tumult of leaves, and lashes to and fro its
branches ; and the blast with its furious trum-
peting comes up the cloven defiles, and strikes
the bare vast slopes of the shorn hills, and, roaring for battle, sweeps thundering down the val-

ley, crowding before it a tumult of cloud and
mist; and from above the heavens themselves
respond with their dread artillery; and, fierce
and swift, the lightning plunges its quivering
blade into the earth, and strikes at random into
the woods, and a great crash is heard as some
tall leader of the forest falls.

Well sheltered, then, in our solid house, we
listen to it as it roars without, and beats and
howls at the windows, and lashes with gusts of
rain the streaming panes, and threatens us vainly
as we sit before our wide chimney, heaped with
logs that the storm itself hath shaken for us to
the ground; and watch the tongues of darting,
passionate fire leap up the black throat of the
chimney, to join the stormy rout; and every
now and then stop in our talk to listen, half in
awe. The Spirit of the Apennines is then worth
communing with. It has many a wild thing
to say that it is well for us to hear — better
than gossip of the city; and where can one hear

it better than here in the heart of Vallombrosa ?——

"When the Apennine walks abroad with the storm."

Then comes the winter. I shall be gone then ; but the poor peasants will stay, and hear what that has to say, when all the world about is covered with its snowy shroud of silence, and far off the valley smiles, like the happy valley of Rasselas ; and they will crowd about their great black-throated chimneys, rough with soot, where blazes their fire of chips and broken brush, and branches gleaned from the wrecks of storm in the forest, and wish and wish, and want, and sigh, and suffer. To me it might have other things to say ; to them it speaks of poverty, of suffering, of hunger, of no work, and, finally, of patience. This is the only flower, perhaps, which will grow for them in winter ; and it is at once one of the most precious and one of the most common flowers that grows in Italy—*pazienza :* and, poor things, they have

need of it here in Vallombrosa. The wonder
is to me to see their patience and their cheer-
fulness under the load they have to bear.

We boast of our civilisation—of the civilisation of Europe and of the nineteenth century.
Alas for our civilisation, as we call it! What
has it done, what does it do, to solve the great
problem of humanity? Is all this poverty,
all this suffering of human beings, helped by
it, or is it caused by it?—that is the question.
Is our so boasted civilisation the world bal-
anced and tottering on its apex, or firmly
settled on its true pyramidal base? Is Liberty
anywhere much more than a name? Is it a
living principle doing good, or a dead pretence?
Was the universal brotherhood of man bound
together by ties of love and animated by pure
and unselfish motives — the grand community
of Christ, where there should be no individual
ownership of property, no selfish abstraction,
and piling up of wealth only a vague and im-

possible dream? Were all His denunciations
of riches empty phrases? Is there, of the
millions who bow down before the altar and
profess themselves Christians, any one who
really believes His doctrines, who is willing
to accept His conditions and renounce all personal wealth? If there be, I do not know him.
Certainly the world is not organised on such
principles. What would Christ say to the present state of things in Europe,—to the mighty
armies and navies that eat out its heart; to the
wars, and bloodshed, and battles for which all
nations are arming and armed; to the enormous
riches piled up in individual hoards; to the
misery and suffering of the poor perishing for
mere want at the doors of the rich. Is Christianity anything more than empty phrases and
dogmas, and long prayers, and phylacteries, and
formal services,—or in our generation do we
pretend to know better than He what is best
and what is practicable? If any one hints at

carrying out His system of universal brotherhood and community of goods, is he not looked
upon pityingly? Do we not shake our heads
wisely at him, and say, "Poor fellow, there is
a bee in his bonnet! It would be better to
put him into an insane asylum"?

Wandering through these woods, where nature preaches her sweet and beautiful gospel,
in these autumnal afternoons, I plagued my
mind with these thoughts; and before I have
finished this little book you will see why I am
thus tormented, and why I foolishly doubt that
perhaps we have not, after all our boasting, and
all our fine words, and all our huzzas for liberty
and union, not only not solved the great problem of government, but perhaps got hold of
it by the wrong end, and why it sometimes
seems to one as if we had organised the devil's
scheme instead of Christ's.

But we will put aside these considerations
for the moment, and yield ourselves up to na-

ture, and bask in the sun, and drink of the
cup of beauty, and enjoy the blessings that
God has given as well as we can.   There may
be a fly in the cup, but no matter.

A beautiful walk of about eight miles carries
us from our lonely house, through exquisite
passages of scenery, through golden chestnut-
groves and solemn fir-forests, to the ancient
monastery of Vallombrosa.   The road com-
mands through its whole course the valley of
the Sieve, and the rolling hills that swell and
sink and rise again in ever-varying lines and
masses, like the heaving of the billows in mid-
ocean, and lift themselves far away against
the horizon.   Thousands of wild flowers smile
along our path.   The wild clematis climbs the
shrubs, and drapes them with its silvery tufts.
The spiring broom clusters everywhere.   The
wild rose, wearing now its coral hips, stretches
and gropes about in the air.   Daisies and

buttercups, purple scabias and **pale pansies,** delicate blue-bells, pale-purple malva, white broad-faced hemlock and silvery thistles, golden arnica, autumnal cyclamen, blue **corn-flowers,** St John's wort, and, in a word, all the common people of the wild flowers, enamel the rough sward. Here, too, long after the summer has passed, still hides in the grass the wild strawberry, for which Vallombrosa was famed of old.[1] At last we come to a small rill, which, tumbling over a rugged shelf of rock, goes its way through a cleft of dark pines down into the plain. This is the Salto del Diavolo, so called; for, as the legend goes, here the good saint Giovanni Gualberto was pursued by Satan, who caught him in his claws and cast him down the declivity. But it is difficult to kill a saint, and he fell unharmed into the valley.

We now descend through a deep dark defile

---

[1] " Et vaga prata ferunt æstu redolentia fraga," says Æmylus Acerbus, in his panegyric of San **Giovanni Gualberto.**

of pines, where the sunshine even at high noon
scarcely penetrates, save here and there to freckle
with spots of light the brown damp carpet,—a
place that recalls that "deep romantic chasm"
of Kubla Khan, "which slanted"

> " Down the green hill athwart a cedarn cover,—
>   A savage place, as holy and enchanted
>   As e'er beneath a waning moon was haunted
>   By woman wailing for her demon lover."

And again climbing, we see before us the noble
old monastery—placed as only the monks knew
how to place a building, and commanding one
of the most magnificent views that can be found
even in this beautiful Italy.   On one side the
sloping hills are dark with miles of serried firs;
on the other, they are golden-brown with glowing
chestnuts; and above, forests of beeches lift their
smooth trunks and climb the mountains.   On
a flat terrace, in the midst of all this, stands the
monastery, a huge square building with inner
courts, in the centre of which is the church, with

its square tower lifting itself above the mass in the sun. In front is an enclosed court, laid out as a garden, and within a wall; and passing out from this through the gateway, we come upon a large enclosed basin of purest water, fed by a perennial and gushing stream, in which the monks of old kept their preserves of trout in prosperous days.

Still beyond are walks through alleys of trees; and on the left, about five hundred paces from the gate, is a fountain which was once thought to possess miraculous powers of healing. " Fontis hujus aqua contra diversos dolores corporis est attributa : ibi blanda medicina confertur, sine tormento cura, sine horrore remedia et sanitas impunita," says Cassiodorus (Variarum, lib. ii. cap. 39). Such was the number of miracles performed by this fountain, that for centuries it was visited by pilgrims, and was held holy, somewhat as the waters of Lourdes are to-day, though by a far more limited number of believers.

Here at this fountain San Giovanni Gualberto,
the founder of the monastery, journeying from
Florence alone in search of some retired hermitage in which to hide himself, paused one summer's day in the year 1008. He was of one of
the most noble and ancient families of Tuscany
—his father, Gualberto Visdomini, claiming to
come from the royal race of the Carlovingians
(the first of his family having been created *cava-
liere* by Charlemagne), and his mother being an
Aldobrandini, of the direct line of Hugo, Duke
of Tuscany. Indeed, according to the historian
Pietro Monaldo, his ancestry went much further
back, even to the times of Catiline, from whom
he directly descended. After that famous con-
spiracy of ancient Rome was foiled by Cicero,
and its chief was driven from the city, two *con-
giunti* of his came to Umbria, and there established themselves. The one who came to
Florence took the name of Visdomini, and was
the ancestor of San Giovanni.

The young Giovanni was brought up in the exercise of arms, and received the education of a gentleman. He was naturally of a fiery disposition. His early manhood had been given to wildness, worldliness, and dissipation at least, if not debauchery, and his conversion to a monastic life was sudden and remarkable. One of his friends, also a Visdomini, in a violent quarrel with his brother Hugo, lost all command of himself, and in a sudden fit of passion plunged his dagger into Hugo's breast and killed him on the spot. Giovanni, furious at his assassination, swore to avenge it. Visdomini fled, and for a time Giovanni pursued him in vain; but at last, on the morning of Good Friday, in the year 1003, as he was going escorted by his bodyguard to Florence, they met in a narrow pathway in the forest, escarped on either side with high rocks, where there was no escape. Drawing his sword, Giovanni told him to prepare for instant death; but his opponent, instead of defending himself, dropped on his knees, and spreading out his arms and hands in the form of a cross, besought Giovanni to remember the day, to spare his life, and to grant him that mercy which otherwise he himself might vainly sué for in another life.   Something there was in the mode of his prayer, and the expression, tone, and attitude of the man, which seemed to have touched to the quick the sensitive spirit of Giovanni, and operated an instant revolution of feeling and purpose.   He forgave him on the spot, assisted him to rise, and dismissed him in safety with his blessing.   He then at once repaired to the neighbouring monastery, at San Miniato, and there prostrated himself before a crucifix in prayer.   As he gazed up, the figure of Christ bent his head to him, as if in approval of his act of clemency.   The miracle so affected him that he at once went to the abbot, solemnly abjured his former life and courses, and begged to enter the confraternity as a brother monk.   The abbot at first refused to receive him, fearing the rage of his father, but finally consented, and Giovanni then took the religious vows in April 1004.

From this time forward he was no longer the same man, but distinguished himself by his humility, piety, and devotion to his new calling, and soon acquired so great a reputation and influence, that on the death of the abbot in 1008, he was unanimously chosen to take his place. This office, however, he could not be induced to accept, declaring himself, in his humility, to be unfitted for it in any way—by all his previous life, by his personal wishes, by his general incapacity to guide others—and stating that his own desire was rather to seek some peaceful and solitary hermitage, where he might spend his life in silent self-communion and prayer, as a hermit, afar from men and from the possibilities of ambition. Filled with these sentiments, he soon after left the convent, and wan-

dering forth on his solitary way from Florence,
ascended the lonely hills of Vallombrosa.   Here,
weary and thirsting from his hot walk, he stopped
beside the fountain which afterwards acquired
such celebrity : the cool waters refreshed him ;
and enchanted by the magnificent prospect
which opened before him, he here determined to
stay, persuaded that this was to be the end of
his wanderings, to which the hand of God had
led him.   The forest gave him shelter and food
sufficient for his wants ; the cool clear spring
poured its perennial waters for his drink ; and
against the fear of serpents and wild animals,
which then infested the woods, he found a defence in prayer.

In the neighbourhood were two hermits named
Paolo and Guntelmo, who had here established
themselves, and were living in two miserable
huts.   These joined him almost immediately ;
and little by little, though against his will at
first—for he desired rather to live in solitude—

there gathered about him a small company of monks and hermits. They built a series of rude huts for shelter—in front of each of which was planted a cross, to conjure away demons and wild beasts—erected in the centre a place of prayer, and enclosed the whole with a circular wooden paling. Among the enemies which surrounded San Giovanni, or which he imagined to surround him, were wild beasts and demons ; but his most serious and palpable foes were the bands of robbers who here found refuge, and who did their utmost to drive him thence by threats and assaults. The little community were beaten cruelly at times, their huts were torn down, and death threatened if they remained. But all was vain. They made no defence, suffered in silence, prayed for their enemies, returned good for evil, fed them in want, tended them when ill, and finally thus overcame them, and were left in peace.

The fame for sanctity of their leader—or pre-

positor, as he was called at first—spread throughout the land. The nobles of the surrounding
country gave him aid and protection, granted
him lands, and advanced him means to build a
church. The Emperor Conrad II., with the
Empress Gisela and all the Court, paid him a
visit, and, touched by the piety and poverty of
the little community, made them large presents.
Gifts and grants of land poured in on all sides.
Among the chief donors may be mentioned
specially the Abbess Itta (head of the convent
of St Hillario or St Ellero); the Counts Guidi,
who were the direct descendants of Otho I., and
the principal owners of the land thereabouts;
afterwards the famous Countess Matilda, who
conferred special honours and grants upon them;
and the republic of Florence, which not only
remitted all taxes upon the monastery, but also
gave lands and favoured it in every way. The
place was then called Acquabella and Acqua-
buona, from the supposed miraculous virtues of

the fountain, and it was not until long after that it received the name of Vallombrosa.

The life led by the monks was half claustral and half eremitical, and their penances and self-inflicted privations almost intolerable. At times they scarcely ate anything, reducing themselves to the point of starvation, and treating even a drink of pure water as a luxury not always permissible. One loaf of bread a-day was divided among three; and often this was made simply of *crusca*, the husks of the grain : and when this was wanting they lived on roots, and wild herbs, and nuts, and whatever they could pick up in the woods. But these penances, they at last found, were beyond human strength and resistance, and they came to the conclusion that God could not require of man more than man could bear. Still they practised extreme abstemiousness, strove in every way to drive out the demon of desire, that, despite their utmost efforts, would possess them, and endeavoured to be chaste, virtuous, and unselfish. Above all, they practised hospitality from the very first, devoting themselves to good offices for the poor, and administering all their means to the succour of the miserable and suffering. One of their penances was to plunge their feet in ice-cold water, and there keep them till they were nearly frozen. And thus, with prayer, reading holy books, fasting, working on the ground, and tending the sick, they passed their lives. Finally, they adopted the complete ordinances of the Benedictines.

The benediction of God, they thought, was manifested to the prepositor, San Giovanni, by a fact they considered miraculous. The tree which grew beside his hut, anticipating the ordinary season, put forth its leaves long before all the others; shaded it during the summer with its abundant foliage; and was the last, when winter came, to shed its leaves on the ground. This was repeated year after year, and was con-

sidered a miracle, so that a wall was built about
the tree, and it was consecrated and held in
highest reverence. This tree was in the year
1008 full-grown; and in 1640, when Diego de
Franchi wrote his 'Life of San Giovanni Gualberto,' it was still flourishing, and a print of it
is engraved in his biography, surrounded by a
wall, and with an inscription. What is supposed to be the same tree, surrounded by a wall
corresponding in appearance to the old print, is
still living and flourishing after these many
centuries.

The monastery grew in numbers and in fame;
and the Countess Matilda, in addition to her
donations, conferred upon the prepositor or prior
—or abbot, as he finally was called—the title
of Count of Magnale,—the same title to pass to
his successors. These donations were confirmed
at a later period by the Emperor Otho IV., who
took the convent under his special protection, and
gave the title of Marchese di Monteverde to the

prior. The original hermitage (Eremo), as it was called, was built in 1015 ; but as time went on, it was repeatedly enlarged and rebuilt. In the fifteenth century the cloisters were increased and a new church erected ; and finally, in 1640, the façade, as it now appears, was added under the pastorate of Don Averardo Niccolini of Florence, and the church and monastery enriched by pictures, statues, codices, engravings, and a large and valuable library.

It is not a matter of any great importance, as far as this little book is concerned, to establish the exact dates of the various events in the life of San Giovanni Gualberto, nor, indeed, would it be easy to do so, as there is a discrepancy in regard to them among the accredited chroniclers of Vallombrosa and biographers of the saint, amounting to nearly thirty years. But in order to avoid the imputation of carelessness on this point, it may be as well briefly to indicate the authorities for the dates I have given.

The historians of the Benedictine Order generally fix the date of the arrival of the saint at
Vallombrosa at 1008, and of the foundation of
the hermitage there at 1015 : Ascanio Tam-
burino states it even earlier, in 1012. Padre
Helyot, however, is of opinion that the establishment of this hermitage could not be earlier
than 1039, and in defending this view he argues
the question at considerable length. The date
of the saint's death in 1073 seems to be well
established, but the date of his birth, and of the
period when he went first to Vallombrosa, is
extremely doubtful,—and on this point the
authorities do not agree. Andrea da Genova,
Taddeo Ademaro, and Diego Franchi agree as
to the date of his death, and say that he was
then eighty years of age. This would fix the
date of his birth at 993 ; but if this be so, he
would have been only sixteen years of age in
1008, when they say that he went to Vallombrosa. This, according to their own dates, must

c

be a mistake, since they affirm that he assumed the monastic dress at eighteen years of age, stayed four years at the convent of San Miniato before going to Vallombrosa, and there remained seven years before building the first hermitage. Giving him one year at Camaldoli, this would have brought him to Vallombrosa in 1016, and fixed the foundation of the hermitage at 1023. Padre Abbate Davanzati (a Vallombrosan) clears up these dates very simply by stating that he was eighty-eight years of age, and not eighty, when he died. This would give his birth at 985, and adding eighteen years—the age at which he took his vows—four years spent at San Miniato, and one year at Camaldoli, would fix his arrival at Vallombrosa at 1008, as they state. Moroni also gives the date of his birth at 985; Padre Soldani, the Vallombrosan, also fixes the date of the first hermitage at 1015, seven years after his arrival, and in this he is supported by various authorities.

Undoubtedly, when the hermitage was first established, there might have been something to fear from the beasts of prey, wolves, and serpents with which the forest then abounded, according to tradition; but besides these, the saint himself declares in a letter—and in this he is upheld by various writers of the period —that terrible voices were heard at night all around them, which they held to be voices of demons, and phantasms of the Evil One; and even a fierce dragon and basilisk threatened their lives. But all these were quelled by prayer, as they were probably evoked by the excitement of the brain and nerves occasioned by too prolonged abstinence from food. The penances and privations of the saint himself were carried to such a point that he was subject to constant fainting-fits, to syncope, and even tetanus, so that his teeth were locked together, and he could only be relieved by prising them apart with a knife, and administering some stimulants. In such a state it is easy to account for all these visions, which were then held to be devilish temptations. More efficacious than his prayers, seems to have been the more generous diet which at last he was forced to take, — condescending under great pressure to add to his nourishment a few ounces more of food, and at times to partake of something cooked, and even to take a fomentation of wine —inasmuch as the Apostle permitted a little wine for the stomach's sake.

The great precepts of the monastery which San Giovanni preached and ordained, were charity and hospitality. In process of time the monastery grew rich with the many donations of the pious, and was enlarged, and increased in influence and in numbers. A hospital was then established for the sick, and for the poor, where medical aid was given and food supplied to those who were in need and suffering. All charities and donations they accepted

in trust for those who were ill and poor; and,
as it would seem, these were administered in a
thoroughly Christian spirit, so that the poor
and sick of all the country about blessed these
monks. Besides this, in the way of hospitality
they gave free lodging and food to all honest
travellers or visitors for three days. The fifth
part of all their revenues they devoted to the
hospital. The laws of their order not permitting
women to enter the monastery, they built a
house expressly for them, for sick, poor, and
visitors, where all the obligations of charity and
hospitality were performed. So the monastery
became celebrated everywhere, and every one
sang its praises. "Vallombrosa," says Ariosto—

> "Vallombrosa, così fù nominata una Badia
> Ricca e bella nè men religiosa,
> E cortese a chiunque vi venia." *

For their motto they had, says De Franchi,
"Obedience to one's elders, community of life

* Cant. 22, st. 36.

and property, concord between the brothers, and love to one's neighbours."

Besides keeping up the monastery at Vallombrosa, the Abbot San Giovanni applied the revenues of this property, which had now become very large, to the erection and establishment of a number of other monasteries under similar regulations, and of restoring still others which had fallen into decay. The utmost efforts of the abbot were specially directed against simony, and to insure decorum and honesty of life and doctrine. Despite his ill-health, he travelled much in search of good works to do, and to succour the poor. "Præcipuus paupertatis amicus" was the title given him by the writers of his time. "Well though he knew that riches are thorns" (*spine*), says De Franchi, "and that it is far better to be without them than not fitly to employ them, he ever feared, although his brethren monks held them in common, that their hearts would be impelled by them to

courses averse from peace and purity. Therefore he resolved to deprive them of a portion of
their riches, reserving only what sufficed for a
tranquil and a happy life, and thus blessing,
with the gifts that they had received from the
laity, the laity and the people. In order to
supply the wants of the needy, he laboured
himself with his old and infirm body to culti-
vate the land and the gardens around, thus
setting an example to all other monks, and
would not allow his own monastery to have
riches which were not used in common and
with humility of spirit." *O si sic omnes!* Well
may we cry with De Franchi, " O vicissitudine
delle antiche virtù! O vestigie smarrite!"

Plague and famine, and earthquake and tempest, at this time came upon Italy, and San
Giovanni made a tour of visits to the various
monasteries subject to his authority, to see that
the hospitals were well furnished, and open to
all who needed aid, reproving severely those in

which he found a surplus of provisions set aside, and praising those wherein the monks had exposed themselves to suffering in order to expend their utmost means in charity. " Cur, inquit, adeo abundamus, cum multos egere videamus ? " To these noble sentiments and acts the world responded, and the more that was given away, the more was brought to his door. One day the monks found themselves without anything to eat except three loaves of bread. By order of the abbot a sheep was killed, and the meat was placed on the table. But all refused to eat of it, and satisfied themselves with the crumbs of bread that remained. The next morning, a number of sacks of corn and grain, and other comestibles, were brought to their gate, and the drivers would say nothing but that it was a gift, sent by gentlemen whom they would not name. The gates of the monastery were then surrounded by the poor, and everything was given away. On another occasion, when the fail-

ure of the harvest had brought much suffering to
the poor, he ordered the granaries of the monastery of St Salvi to be opened, and every one
who was in need to be supplied to the last
grain. In another season of famine he sold all
the sacred vases and utensils of the church,
and all the priestly ornaments and dresses, to
give their proceeds to the hungry. I give these
particulars to show the spirit which animated
this noble abbot; and between then and now
the reader himself may make the comparison,
and see how far we have improved on his
administration.

Many are the miracles attributed to San
Giovanni, but these we will leave aside. The
great miracle was the goodness of the man, and
the noble work he did. In the year 1073 he
died, at the good old age of eighty-eight years.

The same spirit which had animated San
Giovanni continued to govern the Order, and

his memory and precepts were held in highest
honour and reverence. The monastery flourished,
and grew in wealth and territory until it pos-
sessed a vast country, rich in pasture and forest,
keeping up its reputation for charity and hospitality, and affording asylum and sustenance to
all the poor who came to its gates. The land
was well cultivated; the willing labourer always
found work there; and many were the pilgrims
who visited it from all parts of Europe, to all of
whom it accorded a generous hospitality. Here,
among others, came Milton, in the flower of his
youth, to gaze on this magnificent panorama, to
store his mind with images and pictures—that
long remained vivid when the outer windows of
his sight were closed—to study in the library,
to pace the terraces, to ponder the grand poem
of his later years, and to leave behind him a
memory dear to all who love English poetry.
The landscape is still the same as when he saw
it, and the leaves strew the hillsides as thickly

as when he wandered among these shady groves. His shadow walks with every English traveller through the long corridors, where once the monks who are now but dust listened to his silvery tones, and wondered perhaps at this fair youth, with long and golden hair, who came from a far-away country, and spoke softly if brokenly in their native tongue. The charm of this place long lingered in his mind, and he apparently drew upon it for his description of Paradise in his great poem. Already, while pacing these cloisters and woods, he was meditating an epic work, the theme of which was the history of King Arthur and his knights; and in a Latin poem addressed at this time to his friend Manso, Marquis of Villa, he thus alludes to it :—

> " Si quando indigenas revocabo in carmina reges,
> *Arturumque* etiam sub terris bella moventem,
> Aut dicam invictæ sociali fœdere mensæ
> Magnanimos Heroas, et (O modo spiritus adsit)
> Frangam Saxonicas Britonum sub Marte phalanges ! "

This, however, gradually faded from his mind, and gave place to the loftier and grander theme to which he afterwards dedicated his great powers. The impression made by Vallombrosa never left him; and perhaps it was the memory of this lovely landscape, with Florence in the distance, which rose before his blind eyes when he wrote these lines :—

> " As when a scout
> Through dark and desert ways with pain hath trod
> All night, at last, by break of cheerful dawn,
> Obtains the brow of some high-climbing hill,
> Which to his eye discovers unaware
> The goodly prospect of some foreign land
> First seen, or some renowned metropolis
> With glistering spires and pinnacles adorned,
> Which now the rising sun gilds with his beams." *

---

* 'Paradise Lost,' Book iii. 543 ; see also Book iv. 135. So, too, he recalls this spot in his " Epitaphium Damonis," where he says—

> " At jam solus agros, jam pascua solus oberro,
> Sicubi ramosæ densantur vallibus umbræ ;"

or where he speaks of " Flumina, fontesque vagos, nemorumque recessus," in the same poem, his friend Carlo Deodati being the Damon of the poem.

Among the other memories attached to Vallombrosa is that of the monk Guido—commonly
called Guido d'Arezzo or Aretino—to whom we
owe the modern method of notation in music,
the ordination of the gamut, the arrangement of
notes in lines and spaces, and the names *ut, re,
mi, fa, sol, la,* which he first gave to the notes,
and which they still retain. Whether he actu-
ally resided here is open to doubt. Very little
is known accurately in regard to his life. The
dates of his birth and his death are only proxi-
mately established; but he is believed to have
been born towards the end of the tenth century—
in or about 995. It also seems to be established
that he was a monk of Pomposa, and abbot of
some convent,—whether at Camaldoli, Vallombrosa, Sta Croce d'Avellana, or elsewhere in
Italy, Germany, Normandy, is questioned: all
claim him. If he resided at Vallombrosa, it
must have been in the very early days of that
monastery, since the original Eremo was only

built in 1015, and towards the latter part of his life. But whether or not he was here in fact, here he is in tradition at least, and his memory is associated with this place; and here we may fancy him walking through the forests, meditating his musical scheme, and chanting the hymn of San Giovanni, from the first syllables of which he took the names which he gave to the musical notes:—

> *Ut* queant laxis,
> *Re*-sonare fibris,
> *Mi*-ra gestorum,
> *Fa*-muli tuorum,
> *Sol*-ve polluti,
> *La*-bii reatum,
> 　　　Sancte Joannes.

Here also—under the shadows of these trees, and along these hills—might once be seen the august figures of the famous Countess Matilda, the Empress Gisela, the Abbess Itta, the Countess Ermellina; of the Emperors Conrad II., Henry III., and the third and fourth Othos, and long afterwards, Lorenzo the Magnificent; of the Popes Victor II., Alexander II. and IV., Innocent II., Pascal II. (all of whom were monks of Vallombrosa), Leo IX., who made a journey to Vallombrosa expressly to see San Giovanni, and many another Papal figure.

But the most interesting and prominent of all the Papal figures associated with Vallombrosa is that of the famous and haughty Hildebrand, afterwards Gregory VII., who carried the Papacy to its utmost height of domination, triumphed over imperialism, forced Henry to his knees at Canossa, and finally was driven from Rome to end his days at Salerno with the proud and bitter saying, "I have loved justice and hated iniquity, and therefore I die in exile." Here we may see him in imagination traversing the forests alone, and pondering earnestly the future; or accompanied by his devoted patron and friend the Countess Matilda, pausing under the shadows to discuss with her the claims of the Church, and lay out plans for its aggrandisement and purification. Here, according to some historian, it was that he first assumed the monastic robes and took his early vows, before he went to Cluny; and with these murmurous woods his name and his figure are closely associated, at least by tradition.

Various are the accounts as to where he first took orders and made his vows as a monk. The first is that of Ottone Frisonga (1150), Baronius (1048), and Bernried (1120), who assert that it was at Cluny. The second is that of the Bollandists, who say that it was at the monastery of Sta Maria del Monte Aventino at Rome; the third, that it was in Domo S. Petri; the fourth, that it was at the monastery of San Benedetto de Calvello, near Soana; and the last, that it was at the monastery at Vallombrosa. This is directly affirmed, among other writers, by Padre Soldani, himself a learned Vallombrosan monk, in his ' Questioni Vallombrosene ' and his ' Istoria di Passegrano,' and particularly

defended and sustained in an elaborate series of
letters on the subject, in which the whole question is discussed (' Sopra il Monacato e la
Parentela di S. Gregory VII.) His view is
supported by the Sacra Congregazione de' Riti,
which decreed on the 21st of January 1673
that Gregory should be placed in the " Martiro-
logio Romano " for the day of the 25th of May,
under the title of Vallombrosan Monk. Soldani
also asserts that he was related to San Giovanni
Gualberto, which lends probability to his view.
Whatever be the real facts, as we wander
through the woods of Vallombrosa we may,
without fear of critics, give loose to our fancy,
and dream at least that we see that noble figure
of Gregory walking through its meditative paths.

Besides these memories also we may recall
San Pietro Igneo, who here underwent the ordeal
of fire, and passed unharmed through the flames ;
and Beato Tesoro Beccaria, the martyr ; and San
Torello, and San Benedetto Uberto of the royal

D

blood of the Longobards, and many another
priest and monk of note. Here, too, lived the
distinguished botanist Buono Faggi, and Father
Hugford, the English Benedictine, who, in the
last century, revived and improved the art of
imitating marble in scagliola, and specimens of
whose skill still hang on the walls of the monastery; and (as tradition says) Mattio Bandello,
the author of the famous *novelle,* that rival those
of Boccaccio—at least in their looseness, if not
in their style; and here, too, wandered often
Christofano Landino, who wrote the celebrated
comments on Dante, and whose mummied body
may still be seen in the church at Borgo-alla-
Collina, about fourteen miles distant, with this
inscription :—

> " Di Dante, di Maron, del Venosino
>   Quei che seppe spilgar gri alti pensieri
>   Miralo, passegier, quest' è il Landino—
>   D'Ovidio imitò i versi lusinghieri—
>   Spiro nel gran Lorenzo estro divino—
>   Dopo tre scorsi omai secori interi
>   Incorotto lo vedi ; anche il suo frale
>   Par che natura reso abbia immortale."

And here Francesco Berni, coming from his native town of Lamporecchio, meditated those humoristic and sarcastic poems that gave his name in Italy to all similar compositions.

For eight centuries this monastery flourished, and to a certain extent at least preserved its high reputation for charity and hospitality. But in the beginning of the present century a sad change came over its fortunes. The first bolt of doom fell upon it when Napoleon in 1810 swept away with a rude conquering hand the right of ecclesiastical property, confiscated most of the conventual houses, seized their possessions, and drove the monks forth to seek what refuge they could in the world. Vallombrosa was not excepted from his ban. The monastery and church were despoiled of their treasures. Its large domains were seized, and the monks themselves were forced to abandon the asylum which had been the home of their order for centuries.

After the fall of Napoleon, when Austria resumed its sovereignty in Tuscany, the monks were reinstated as far as possible by Leopold in their rights and possessions, and again returned to the monastery. A considerable portion of their lands had, however, in the meantime, been sold, and passed into the hands of other proprietors, and this could not be reclaimed. Still a large part of it remained, and this again became theirs. Their return was welcomed by all the neighbourhood, and especially by the peasants and the poor, who all had felt the benefit of their charity, and many of whom had earned their living by labour on the land. They administered the property well, and the large profit it yielded seems to have been devoted to good ends. The poor and disabled found always at the convent doors their soup and bread. The able-bodied were hired to work in the fields, to tend the cattle and herds, to cut the trees, to gather the dead wood or the fruits of the forest, and thus they earned a fair living. If ill, they were taken care of, and found beds in the hospital, and fitting medicines, free of expense.

The number of monks was in later times about 150, varying a little from year to year. Their lives were not as empty as the lives of most monks are ; for besides their religious exercises and their studies, from which latter no particularly valuable literary results seem to have been derived, they had other outdoor duties and amusements to occupy their time and their minds.

Mounted on their donkeys or the small nervous horses of the Maremma, they made their rounds of the woods and fields to superintend the farms, the forests, the herds ; or with their guns on their shoulders, and accompanied by their dogs, they pursued the game with which the place abounded.

The austerity of the early days declined as time went on, though the strict rules of the

order were kept. One particular penance, however, they always continued to practise. This
was to rise at one o'clock every morning, and go
from their cells to the church, there to recite
their prayers. The monks were genial and
kindly to the peasants, and to all with whom
they had intercourse, and they were universally
liked. The scandal is—and it may be nothing
but scandal—that they did not all observe very
strenuously the strict laws of that chastity which
in earlier days was enforced; and it was the
belief that they were the fathers of many of the
children in the neighbourhood, particularly in
the little village of Tosi. Whether this be true
or not, it did not at all embitter their relations
with the fathers, husbands, or brothers: all was
certainly taken in good part, and if anything
was to be forgiven, it was forgiven and smiled
at. Certain it is, that whatever of this kind
may have occurred, it was quite exceptional to
the character and habits of the main body of

the brothers, who led a simple dignified life, and were anything but idle and useless members of society.

Besides all the rest of their duties, they occupied themselves in public instruction, and founded at the monastery a seminary or college for the education of young men of rank. The Rev. John Chetwood Eustace, in his ' Classical Tour through Italy,' who visited the convent in the early part of this century, about the year 1810, characterises this seminary as "excellent." " Many of the Florentine youth of rank," he says, "were there at the time of our visit. Their dress is a black gown with a black collar lined and edged with white. We were present at one of their amusements, which was the Calcio or Balloon, a game of great repute both in Italy and France. Their looks and manners seemed to display the advantages, both physical and moral, of the situation."

The old belief of San Giovanni and his

brother hermits as to the wild beasts, basilisks,
and demons that haunt the place, does not,
apparently, seem to have entirely died out even
at the period when Mr Eustace paid his visit
to the monastery. One of the " good fathers,"
in conversation with him, told him that "during
the winter, which commences here in October
and lasts till May, they were buried in snow
or enveloped in clouds, and besieged by bears
and wolves prowling round the walls and in
the forests. ' *Orsi, lupi, e tutte le peste,*' was his
emphatic expression." I am afraid the good
father drew largely on his imagination, or on
the credulity of his listener, in these statements.
I have just been in Vallombrosa in late October, and never was there a scene more enchanting and genial. The leaves were thick on the
trees, and the country smiling with flowers.
As for the *orsi, lupi, e tutte le peste,* I saw none,
I heard of none,—unless the good father considered women as coming under the last classi-

fication, **and** the Government guards under **the** first, and mistook the foxes for wolves.

Before the monastery was despoiled **it pos-sessed a** remarkably interesting library, contain-ing a considerable number of **rare** and valuable ancient manuscripts, **and** rich **in** ecclesiastical works. These, however, **were** piled pell-mell together and carried away exposed **in carts,** some here, some there. Many, **of** course, **were** lost; **but** what remains of them **are** now de-posited **among the** national archives in Florence. **Their** paintings, some of which were **of** rare excellence; their treasures of plate; **their elabo-**rately embroidered vestments and altar-cloths; their sculptured figures **in** silver or terra-cotta, among which **were some** admirable bassi rilievi by Luca della Robbia,—were **all** taken, **and the greater** part of them carried to Paris **or sold.**[1]

[1] " The pictures, designs, and **engravings**" (says **Fontani** in his 'Viaggio Istorico Pittorico **dell' Italia,'** p. **160, 1818),** " were numberless, and even to cite them, and enumerate in-

Their museum of mineralogy, which, for the period and place, was considerable, was not only scattered, but the specimens they had collected were thrown away by the roadside or in the woods as of no value, and even to the present day they are occasionally unearthed. Their pharmacy, which was celebrated, was also broken up; and a very considerable number of the beautiful old majolica vases with which it was furnished were found only last year 'in an antiquary's shop, and sold for almost nothing. In a word, the monastery was not only despoiled, but despoiled in the most reckless way: of all its treasures, nothing, or almost nothing, now remains.

On the return of the monks from their exile,

dividually one by one their merits, would be an extremely long and tiresome task. The library was rich in works adapted to sacred study, and in the learned languages, as well as in subjects relating to art and to modern philosophy. It contained also rare editions, especially of the fifteenth century, and valuable manuscripts, rich with beautiful ornamentation and miniatures."

the Grand Duke Leopold did what he could to
reinstate them in their possessions; but much
was irrevocably lost. Of the land, as I have
said, a considerable portion has been **sold**; **and**
dotted here **and** there over this property **are**
little fragments and corners of land owned by
private persons, generally peasants. Their landed
property, however, was still very extensive and
productive. Taxes then in Tuscany were very
light; for the Government was inexpensively
conducted, the country was prosperous, the revenues large, the Grand Duke paternal **in** his
rule, the court simple, industry flourishing, and
the cost of living slight in comparison with what
it now is. Whatever political griefs the Tuscans
may have had to complain of, they **were not**
oppressed by taxes and Government impositions
as they now are. **As the** annual taxes on this
property were 29,000 *scudi*, **it is plain** that
the revenues **it** yielded **must** have **been very**
large. Reckoned at **6 per cent, they would**

have amounted to 400,000 *scudi*, which is more than 2,000,000 francs.

How, then, was this revenue obtained? In the first place, from the forests, which yielded an immense supply of timber, that in itself was very valuable for building—being principally of chestnut, beech, and firs. What was not fitted for this purpose served as firewood. Again, the fruit of the chestnuts, enormous in quantity, brought in a very considerable sum. A great saw-mill, run by water-power, was in constant operation; and this alone, it was calculated, paid the Government tax. Besides this, herds of cattle and flocks of sheep were pastured here, and bred. One great farm, called the Mettata, was devoted to dairy purposes, and housed a hundred cows; another, the Porcaria, was a farm for pigs. Still others were sown with grain; and though a good deal of the land was wild and unproductive, yet a large portion was fairly well cultivated. To carry on all this a

great number of persons was required ; and all
the labouring population found their benefit
from it, as well as the towns and cities, which
were thus supplied with food, and fruit, and
timber.

This state of things continued until Tuscany
renounced, by popular vote, its autonomy, and
annexed itself to Piedmont and the young king-
dom of Italy.   Then came the abolition of the
monastic houses, and the expropriation of all
their property; and Vallombrosa, among the
rest, became the public domain.   The monks
were driven away, and the property is now
administered by the Italian Government.

For one, on principle, I protest against this
violent assumption by the Government—this
expropriation, without fair remuneration, of monastic property.   It is a clear violation of all
rights of property, or all so-called rights admitted and established by the consent of all

civilised nations, for *ab origine* the only right is
force,—

> " That they shall take who have the power,
>   And they shall keep who can."

If a Government can sequester and assume at
its will, without payment therefor, all property
belonging to religious bodies and communities,
why can it not, on the same principle, take
the property belonging to any other class
or corporation — to merchants, to artists, to
princes, to hospitals, to colleges? Of course,
it is admitted by established laws that it may,
for the public necessity or benefit, take any
private property, but solely on one condition,
that it gives a fair remuneration for it; and this
is precisely what it does not do in the case of
monastic bodies. If monastic institutions are
contrary to what are deemed the best interests
of the State, it may abolish them; it may pro-
hibit the establishment of such bodies for the
future; it may possibly even break up those that

exist: granted, but only on the same conditions which would apply to all other property held by all other bodies. There cannot justly be one law for monks and nuns as to property, and a totally different one for all other persons. This would be simply a tyrannical exercise of power, contrary to all equity, contrary to all recognised principles of law. In the case of religious corporations, their lands and houses have been given, granted, or purchased by them according to law; and it is impossible to see why they should be made an exception to all other persons, why their lands should be virtually wrested from them without adequate remuneration, and why they should be turned out into the world on a scanty pittance, scarcely sufficient to enable them to live. It is even worse in some respects for them than for any other class; for their vows, and habits of life, and religious pledges, not only render them unfit for other avocations, but disable them from assuming them. I have no special admiration for or sympathy with monastic bodies. They have undoubtedly done good work in the past, and in their monasteries for centuries was kept alive the fire of literature, which was elsewhere almost entirely extinguished. Without them a gross darkness would have covered the world; the precious works of ancient learning would have been lost; science would have suffered total eclipse, and civilisation declined. If there was a good deal of superstition mixed up with their religious doctrines, if their lives were not on the highest line of Christianity, their influence was at least humanising. They afforded refuge and succour to the poor; they exercised the duties of hospitality; they preached and practised charity to their neighbours, and held up a higher standard of life. They showed at times rare examples of piety and good works; and at all events, whatever were their short-comings, they were above the general level of society. Their lands and houses were solemnly and formally given to them by deed or bequest. They were as absolute owners of them by law as any other persons or bodies were of their houses and lands : and if it is now thought, on the whole, that their good work has been accomplished, and their influence is noxious, this may be a good reason, even if it be a mistaken one, for abolishing them as corporations, and restricting their powers and rights for the future ; but it is not a good reason for depriving them of their possessions without proper remuneration, and making them exceptions to the laws applying to all other persons and property. Liberty and law in a properly administered country are universal in their operation. It is not one thing for one class and another for another class.

But Italy has thought differently, and has abolished most of the monastic orders, and confiscated the greater portion of their property, without that fair remuneration which would have been denied to no other class; and in its estimation, as Hosea Biglow says—

> "Libbaty's a kind of thing
> That don't agree with niggers"

—or monks. Among other monasteries, Vallombrosa has been confiscated; and of the hundred monks who have lived and administered this large property, and studied and performed the duties of hospitality and charity, only three now remain—on sufferance—deprived of all rights of ownership.

The question is, on the whole (without regard to the justice and equity of the change), What advantage has been gained by the nation—the people at large—or the people and peasants of the neighbourhood? In the matter of revenue, the nation has certainly been the loser. As we have already seen, under the administration of the monks the taxes then paid to the Government, light as taxes were then, amounted to 29,000 *scudi* or *francesconi*—equivalent to about

125,000 francs in gold—all of which was derived from the profits of one great saw-mill. At
present the net income of the entire property
is about 45,000 *lire* or francs in paper, at a
discount of from 10 to 12 per cent, or about
60,000 in gross. The annual loss, then, is at
least from 65,000, taking the gross revenue, to
80,000, taking the net revenue, as we properly
should.

What advantage has been derived by the people,
and the peasants and labouring classes of the
neighbourhood, the latter of whom depended on
it for their living? Absolutely none, and worse
than none. The saw-mill exists no longer: it
has been done away with. There is absolutely
no tillage or cultivation of the land, which lies
dead and unproductive, save in its growth of
forest-trees. The solid stone farmhouses are all
untenanted, and falling to ruin daily, save one or
two which are inhabited by the guards of the
forest. One of these (called the Mettata) is the

remnant of what was formerly the centre of a large dairy-farm, and gave stabling to some hundred cows. But no cows pasture there now on the grassy slopes from which not even the hay is mown ; and the greater part of the house was torn down by order of the Government a couple of years ago—for what reason it is difficult to imagine, as it was strongly built of solid stone, and would have stood there even if left alone for a century. The farm of the Porcaria (or Porcheria, as it is now more fitly called), where herds of pigs were kept, and yielded a large profit, is abolished, and the building is untenanted. Here and there are to be seen small plantations or nurseries of young trees ; and this is all that is now cultivated on these miles of magnificent country. No cattle are seen or allowed ; no flocks of sheep ; no fields of grain ; no cultivation of any kind, save a few small plantations of infant trees. All the revenue is

given by nature, almost without the assistance
of man. One house alone, called the Lago, has
been reclaimed; and this was the old hunting-
box of the Medici, which my friends have taken
on lease, and repaired and put into habitable
condition ; but even this the Government despoiled of its old castellated towers, which lent
a picturesque and medieval character to the
building. The Casetta, another old stone house,
with large farms connected with it, is also utterly
deserted and left to its fate. All that remains
of its former cultivation is a small patch of plantation in front. Standing there, what a magnificent prospect opens before the eye !—over the
turbulent rolling waves of mountains, which lie
below for many a mile basking in the sunshine,
with little valleys scattered here and there, dot-
ting the distant slopes, and Pontassieve clinging
to the river-banks; and Florence, far beyond,
with its towers and domes; and armies of firs

and chestnuts and beeches crowding up the hillsides; and the blue smoke of charcoal-burners
winding up into the tender sky; and the rugged
fields alive with wild flowers—ferns, gorse, and
broom.

All these farms, and fields, and herds, and
forests once furnished work for the labourer and
the farmer and the peasant; and their life was
thus rendered comparatively easy and happy.
Now there is nothing for them to do or to gain,
and they are very poor and miserable. All the
natural products of the woods and fields are
farmed out, after the usual custom of the Government, at an annual rate. These are the
chestnuts which heap the ground in the autumn,
and the brushwood and *débris* of the forest; and
only what is left of gleaning, after the harvest,
is allowed to the poor, who even pay for this a
very small price. On these gleanings, for the
most part, they live. And every day in the
autumn you will meet them gathering the few

chestnuts which remain on the ground, and
tying together fascines of small brushwood, and
broken sticks, with which to warm themselves
and cook their poor fare in winter. Once in a
while they get a little work and a few *sous* to
eke out their small store. During the summer
they get along fairly well. The climate is
kindly, and the woods supply them with berries,
especially with raspberries and wild strawberries,
which here grow in great abundance, and which
they gather and sell. In the autumn there are
thousands of mushrooms of every kind, which
they gather and carry to the villages and towns,
and there sell for almost nothing to dealers, to
be sent to the city. These mushrooms are de-
licious, and some of them so large and succulent
that one of them makes a dish by itself. Besides the common kind known to us, there are
the large orange-hued *ovole*, the delicate foliated
alberetti, the lilac-grey *porcini*, and many another,
which we class among the foul funguses, avoid

.   as poisonous, and call by the opprobrious name
of toad-stools.[1]

These poor people rarely taste of meat,—it is
too expensive.   Their chief food is a sort of
heavy bread made of dry and ground chestnuts,
or a kind of coarse grain, with beans, roots, or
fruits which they find in the woods, the nuts of
the beech, and potatoes when they can afford to
buy them.   Nor have they much even of this
fare.   How they manage to live on it is to me
a mystery; and a still greater mystery it seemed

---

[1] All the slopes of the Apennines abound in mushrooms,
some of which are of very large size.   Soldani, in his ' Guida
storica,' says that in the neighbourhood of Camaldoli there is
a certain kind of fungus called Vesce di Lupo, globular in
shape, and white within and without, which attains the weight
of 24 Italian pounds; and he adds, in confirmation of his
statement, the fact that a certain Padre Don Adelelmo, a Cam-
aldolese monk, made him and his uncle a present of one of
these Vesci, which, when whole, weighed 21 lb., and that
he and his family ate it and found it excellent.   This mushroom is probably the same as that described by Theophrastus
(Hist. Plant., lib. i. cap. 9) as the Cranium, on account of its
resemblance to the human skull.   Marsili also describes a
mushroom which grows near Padua, along the Euganean Hills,
which sometimes weighs 25 lb.

when they showed me the small store of their gleanings of chestnuts which they had laid up for their winter supply. Still, with all their privations, they look strong and healthy. The children were rosy and vigorous, the maidens some of them handsome, and all well-grown and erect. So also the young men were fine-looking, stalwart fellows. But age soon tells upon them; they grow old early; and when disease strikes them, they have little powers of resistance. On all their faces, after they had passed thirty, there was the pinched, sad look of patient poverty, and a certain refinement, too, of expression in their worn faces, as well as great gentleness of manner and speech—at least among those whom I saw and to whom I spoke—that awakened sympathy and respect. None of them begged, though it was plain that they were in need.

I was speaking of them one evening as we were sitting round our dinner-table, when the

Marquis Fornace said of some of the peasant girls,—" All are remarkably handsome, or rather, I should say, were, for I only knew the place years ago. Beppa, for instance. Beppa was a great beauty. Do you remember Beppa?" turning to our host.

"Beppa? of course I do. She was born in this very house where we are now living; and as I used frequently to shoot over this ground years ago, when I was a bachelor, many a night I have passed here when she was growing up into a woman. Yes, she was handsome."

"Handsome? she was magnificent! What eyes! dark and luminous, and clear as an autumn night. Then what teeth! the pearls of Marchesini were nothing beside them. What a smile! What a figure, lithe as a willow, and full of grace! Ah, what a beauty!"

"Poet!" cried our host — "poet! He exaggerates, as all poets do. Still, there is some foundation in fact for what he says. Beppa

had fine **eyes** and superb **teeth,** I admit, **and**
was **a very pretty** girl. **Of course,** she **was**
slender, but **she was young ;** and **all** the women
here are slender. Elvira, her sister-in-law, was
really a beauty, **and** had **one of** those **Madonna**
faces such **as** Raffaelle delighted to paint, such
as any painter might rejoice **to have as a model**
—simple, **sweet,** refined, and peaceful."

"**Ah ! I never saw her,**" said the Marquis ;
" **but I** daresay **she** was **all you** describe her to
be. But Beppa, Beppa **was my beauty.**"

" **What there was besides** her **eyes** and teeth
that was charming **in** Beppa was **a fine careless-**
ness and thoughtlessness **of** bearing, **a** certain
frank light-hearted way she **had in** all **her**
movements and speech—a sort of freedom, like
a wild natural thing that **the** world had **not**
tamed."

" **Do you** remember," said the Marquis, " **that**
little expedition **we** made together **years ago**
(how the years go ! **it must be at** least twelve

—more, perhaps ; and it seems scarcely six
months !)—in May, I think, or it might have
been later in the year ?   Janet was with us,
and the M.'s, and we set out from Vallombrosa
to walk to Poder Nuovo and picnic in the
woods ; and as we were coming up the rough
road, a little way from the Lago, suddenly
' Poum, poum ' above us roared the thunder like
a broadside of a hundred guns, and the heavens
seemed to split open, and down came the rain
in a deluge.   When it rains in this country, it
rains—it does not make believe.   Fortunately
we all of us, save you, had umbrellas and water-
proofs, and so we were protected ; but you, after
the foolish way you always had, scorned such
impedimenta—and there you were, with nothing
to shield you, saying you did not care for
such trifles.   Well, in a few minutes you were
drenched to the skin, and dripping as a drowned
rat, and we were all of us glad to find a refuge
here at the Lago.   There and then it was that

I first saw Beppa, standing in the doorway, and
inviting us to come in for shelter. Glad enough
we were to accept her smiling invitation, and in
we went. She piled up in the vast fireplace
a heap of dry fascines and broken boughs, and
in a few minutes broad quivering sheets of flame
flashed and roared up the chimney, and we all
gathered about it to dry ourselves. But you
were too thoroughly drenched to be dried in
this way, and cried out to Beppa, who was
bustling about, and laughing with us, and finding us chairs and benches, and helping the
ladies—'Beppa, I say, I must take off these
clothes to be dried. Is there nothing you can
give me to put on while they are drying—no old
coat or cloak of the *babbo's?*—no matter what.'

"'Nothing, signor, nothing—unless you will
put on one of my dresses,' laughed Beppa. 'If
that will do, it is quite at your service; but I
am afraid that will not do.'

"'And why not?' you cried. 'It will do

capitally, if you will lend it to me. *Presto !
presto !* let me have it !'

"' *Davvero,*' said Beppa, ' really you are jok-
ing.'

"' Not a bit of it,' you cried ; ' not a bit of
it ! Let me have it. *Via !* '

" Beppa entered into the joke at once, and
off you and she went ; and then she returned,
shrugging her shoulders and laughing. After a
short time, in you came. *Madonna mia,* what
a figure you were, dressed in one of her gowns !
I never shall forget it. We welcomed you with
shouts, and laughed till we could laugh no
longer for very pain ; and Beppa clapped her
hands, and bent herself down to the ground
with laughing, and spread herself against the
wall, utterly overcome with the joke. What a
mad company we were ! *Per Bacco !* these were
glorious days ! Then we put some chestnuts
in the ashes to roast, and talked and chattered
while the storm passed by. What a picture it

was — worthy the brush of Rembrandt in its effects! The fire darting its quivering tongues up the chimney, redly illuminating our faces and figures, and gleaming on the black rafters overhead; the shadows on the old walls, wavering about as we moved; the faint light of the day, peering through the small iron-barred windows; and then the peals of thunder, echoing along the hills as the storm wore away! It was a scene not to forget. That was my first acquaintance with Beppa. Where is she now? What has become of her?"

"Ah!" said our hostess, "I am afraid the after-acts of the play do not quite correspond to the first bright scenes. Poor Beppa! all that gay spirit has been quenched out of her life. She laughs very little, I am afraid, now."

"I am sorry to hear it," said the Marquis. "Pray tell me what has happened to her."

"She had her love-story—and a pretty one enough it was—and all seemed to go with her 'merry as a marriage-bell.' Her lover and husband was a strong handsome fellow, with no means except his stout arms; and with these he managed to support her—not well, of course, but sufficiently—for their wants were small, and they were fairly happy and contented. But, somehow or other, he did not get on well with the guards of the forest; and there was bad blood between them. So they tracked and watched him to catch him in some violation of the forest-laws, so as to put the hand of the law on him. Unfortunately, whether by mistake or not I cannot say, he took away some brushwood and dead branches of no sort of value, but which were within prohibited limits. He did not, however, take them for himself—he brought them to us, supposing that they were thrown away and useless; and this proves that he had no intention at least of stealing. But here was a chance for his enemies; and he was at once arrested and thrown into prison on an accusation of theft. My husband, on being informed of it,—what did you do ? You know better than I."

" I went down to Figline, where the poor fellow was imprisoned, and did all that I could to free him from the imputation — declaring that I had known him and employed him even in matters of trust, and had found him scrupulously honest as far as I knew, and urged that the very fact of his not having taken the wood for himself was a clear proof that he did not intend to steal. I was fortunate enough to prevail, and he was set free."

" And not an hour too soon," said our hostess. " Poor Beppa, who was then close on her confinement, had wept her heart away during the month that he was in prison. She was alone with scarcely any means of subsistence. Her husband could earn nothing for her, and was besides under accusation of a crime which would probably be fatal to his and her future. She had four children to look after and support.

F

What could he or she do, even if he were liberated? It was a terrible blow. Two days after his return she gave birth to her fifth child."

" And now how is it with them?" said I.

" You shall see them to-morrow. Of course, since this affair all is dark with them. He can find no occupation here, and they all have to suffer."

So we went to see her in her wretched house. Suffering and privation and toil had made her old before her time. Remains of beauty certainly were there. The eyes and the teeth still were beautiful. But the face was haggard and thin, and very sad, and the joyousness and spring of life and youth utterly gone. Still the old sweet smile gleamed for moments over the face, and then faded into sadness again. One of her children was ill and in bed; the others, strong, nut-brown, with large lustrous eyes, stood beside her, shy, silent, half clothed, but with no shadow of care upon their faces. We talked a little with her; and our hostess told her to come up to the house the next day, and she would give her something to keep her children warm for the winter. I gave them a few pennies meanwhile, and then we said good-bye. She thanked us, looked at us with a strange pathetic look, and then burst into tears.

The next day she came to us, with a girl, of about six years of age; and the two rosy, sunny-haired, blue-eyed children of my hostess, with their little arms full of thick stuffs for winter clothing, stood beside their mother, and each saying, "*A te*," thrust them into the hands of the peasant girl, and then stood still and stared at her. She, shy and not knowing what to do, took them almost mechanically; but when her downcast eyes fell upon them, a flash of joyous light went over her face, but she said nothing. "Say *Grazie*," said the mother,— "*grazie, signora; grazie, signorine.*" "*Grazie, signora,*" repeated the child, as if she were saying a lesson. "Hold up your head," said Beppa; "don't look down so and stick out your stomach, but look up." The little one lifted up her head a moment, and dropped it again. What she said when she got away and found her tongue, one can easily imagine; but there she was too shy to speak. It was a pretty picture, and a characteristic scene.

The next day another little one came—by request — and alone, to have a similar gift. This little maid, with eyes black as sloes, and thick tangled hair, of about seven, was as a little mother to the four younger children, and took care of them with a patience, intelligence, and sense of responsibility which was remarkable. It is only among the poor that such precocity is found; but here in Italy, duties and responsibilities and family cares are thrown upon young children at an age when among richer classes they would be thought too young to be left alone. Here, however, they not only have to take care of themselves, but to look after their younger brothers and sisters—and this little maid was as serious and trustworthy almost as a grown woman. She gathered the chestnuts and brushwood; knew all the mushrooms that were edible, and where the strawberries and raspberries grew, and what she could take and what she must avoid; and kept all the little ones in order and out of danger, and carried them when they were tired, and soothed them when they cried, and assisted her mother in household affairs, and was, in a word, a little woman.

The Government is now building a road from Vallombrosa to unite it with the highroad leading from Pontassieve, and this during the summer has afforded work for the people in the vicinity. But suddenly, by order from head-quarters, a stop was put to all this work a month ago, and all the labourers were thrown out of employ, and the little wages they hoped to gain thereby to keep them comfortably through the winter are cut off, so that there is rather a dreary prospect before them. The wages paid here for a day's labour are only 1 franc, 20 centimes; but this satisfies them if it only continues, so that they can count upon it. But when they are cut off from this, their chances are poor enough. As this is the only employment given to them by Government for years (except in the case of the six forest-guards, who have a monthly pay), this sudden stoppage of work is disastrous to these poor people, who have few other means of earning a livelihood.

The Tuscan peasants, both men and women, are almost invariably dry, thin, and spare in their build—seldom becoming fat, as is the case with the Romans and Neapolitans, even among the peasantry—and not having the appearance of great vigour. But in fact they are capable of much endurance; and though, like all Italians, rather indolent by temperament, and needing some spur to action, they are not only active and strong, but have great powers of resistance in their work. "Strong! I think so," said our host. "I will give you an example. Last year I bought of the Government five thousand pounds of charcoal, made by the charcoal-burners in the woods of Vallombrosa, about three miles from my house. Those I hired three men and two women to bring to me—over a rude and difficult path. Within six hours, during one of which they rested to take their mid-day meal and siesta, every stick of it was deposited in my cellar—all carried by them on their heads. The day was extremely hot—and you should have seen them as they came in, erect as masts and bearing their monstrous burdens aloft, and swinging along with a firm and even step down the rough slopes. One of these women in especial roused my admiration. She was a per-

fect gipsy in appearance, with ruled brows, black
eyes, a wealth of wild tangled waving hair that
strayed loosely over her shoulders, and a com-
plexion dark enough in itself, but blackened to
coal with the charcoal-dust which sifted over
her; her arms and legs were bare; her eyes like
fire; down her cheeks rolled great broad streams
of sooty perspiration; and through her parted
lips her white teeth almost shone as she came
up panting and smiling. She was a striking
creature in every way. With twenty baths of
hot water and a clean fresh dress, instead of the
worn, flimsy, and shabby rags which scarcely
covered her, she would have made an impression
anywhere, with her stately figure and her wild
handsome face; but for me, I preferred her as
she was, and I only wished I were an artist to
paint her, with her charcoal burden, her clinging
rags, her grimed face and arms, her bare feet,
her streaming hair—all, in a word, just as she
was."

The villagers of Raggioli and Tosi, and others in the vicinity, live entirely on what they gather in the woods during the summer and autumn. Before daybreak — by three in the midsummer mornings — they are up and off, with their baskets poised on their heads, their blue and purple dresses, a red or party-coloured handkerchief drawn across their brows and knotted behind, and another folded Vandyke-wise over their shoulders. All day long they wander, and pluck the blackberries, strawberries, raspberries, mushrooms, or whatever the woods afford according to the season, and carry home at night their store, to be bought by dealers for the cities and large towns. These natural fruits of the soil the Government allows them to gather (except the chestnuts) free of tax; and as they are very abundant, and largely in demand, they thus gain a little money to support themselves.

A short distance above the monastery rises a steeply scarped rock, at one side of which pours down, roaring and foaming, the torrent of Vicano; and on the summit of this, 1027 metres above the sea and 70 metres above the monastery, stands the so-called Oratorio of the Paradisino. This was originally founded by Padre Biagio Milanese, General of the Order of the Benedictines, as a place of refuge, retirement, and discipline, to which those monks who had offended against the rules of the monastery, or who were under penance, self-inflicted or imposed upon them, retired from time to time, and there led a life more rigorous and disciplinary than the other monks. The prospect from here is wider and even more magnificent than that of the monastery below, overlooking the vast valleys and slopes from the chain of Etruscan mountains which rises against the horizon on the north, to the hills of Leghorn that skirt the Mediterranean. A steep and rugged climb carries us to the summit, where the *celle* and church and tower stand. The church formerly contained some valuable pictures, among which may be mentioned one of Andrea del Sarto's finest works. But it is now despoiled of all its pictures and wood-carving, and is used as a magazine, barn, or hay-loft. The old mill, once driven by the Vicano, is still standing; but it is no longer used, as it was by the monks, to saw trees or to grind corn; nor are the *ghiacciaie*, or ice-basins, turned to any purpose.

Near the monastery is another low building called the Foresteria, which was built to receive women who came to visit the monastery. Originally, by the rules of the Vallombrosa order, no woman was allowed to enter the forest, or to pass within some large crosses erected at a distance of about a quarter of a mile. This rule was enforced for some eight centuries, but afterwards was relaxed; and the Foresteria was built to afford lodging for female visitors. It is now used as an inn, and is crowded with visitors during the summer, who come to breathe the refreshing air, and to enjoy the prospect and the delightful walks which extend in every direction.

A four-miles walk down through the woods carries us to Paterno, which also formerly belonged to the monks and was attached to the monastery. Here originally stood a castle of the Counts Guidi, and was granted by them, with all the circumjacent land, at a very early period to San Giovanni and his brotherhood. Here came Otho III., weary of life and tormented with remorse for the cruel murder of Crescentius, to expiate his offence by penance; and here, according to some of the old chroniclers, he met his death, poisoned by Stephania, the widow of Crescentius, whom he had afterwards made his mistress. The castle was at a later period turned into a monastery, and suffered many changes to adapt it to their use. At present it is a large, square, strong-built conventual edifice of stone, commanding a beautiful view, and surrounded by extensive grounds, and farms, and meadows. These were once admirably cultivated by the monks, and were covered with fields, vineyards, and olive-orchards, which yielded a large revenue, and supplied them abundantly with oil, wine, and grain. A good deal of oil (according to Vallisnieri) was also extracted from the beech-nuts; and Dr Giov. Targioni Tozzette has written three papers on this subject, urging that this oil is not only good for burning, but has very valuable medicinal properties. Besides this, the beech-nuts were largely used by the monks for food for their animals, and especially for their pigs, of which they had a large number.

Among the memories connected with this place is that of Gerbert, afterwards Sylvester II., the companion and friend of the first two Othos, and the preceptor of the young and brilliant Otho III., who here came to such an untimely end. The letters of Otho to Gerbert breathe the warmest affection and respect; and well was he deserving of it, both for the excellence of his character and his wonderful attainments. In any age he would have been a remarkable man, but in the darkness of this century he shines like a great light against the sombre background of its superstition and ignorance. Such was his superiority in point of learning to those by whom he was surrounded, that he was popularly supposed to have obtained his great knowledge at the expense of his soul, and to have been in league with the Evil One. He seems to have been an almost universal genius—distinguishing himself as a poet, a musician, a mathematician, a phy-

sician, an inventor in mechanics, and an author
in various branches of science and literature,
metaphysics, grammar, rhetoric, philosophy, theology, geometry, astronomy, arithmetic, and al-
gebra; and besides all this, to have fulfilled
with dignity and honour his functions as Pope,
and to have been a peacemaker between the
various and agitating factions of the day.
Among his inventions were a hydraulic organ,
in which the amount of air necessary to produce
the sound was effected by steam; and a famous
celestial sphere and solar clock. He is also
supposed by some writers to have invented the
first clock which went with wheels, and the
method of escapement. This is, however, doubtful; and the better opinion seems to be that we
owe this to the Archdeacon Pacifico in the ninth
century. However this may be, he improved
certainly upon it, and has the reputation of
being the first who made a clock to strike the
hours. He first introduced into Europe the use

of the Arabic numerals, and the decimal system. His treatise on geometry is clear and precise; he was a good Greek scholar, and a master of the Latin language, in which he wrote various poems; he was also an admirable musician, and a composer, among other things, of *cantici spirituali,* some of which are still preserved among the monuments of the Liturgy for their beauty.

Here at Paterno he often came—in company with Otho his pupil, and alone—and here he presided over a famous synod to compose the differences between Welligiso di Magonza and Bernward of Hildesheim as to their jurisdiction over the convent of nuns at Hildesheim. Among the other famous figures might then be seen here the noble Abbess Gerberga, sister of Otho II., then old and inform, who warmly espoused the cause of Bernward; and her rival and niece Sophia, the eldest sister of Otho III., proud and ambitious, and daily acquiring influence, who took vehemently the part of Welligiso. Earnest almost to fierceness were the passionate debates that there took place, and it needed all the influence of Gerbert to prevent an open outbreak: even as it was, the synod was forced to adjourn without composing the quarrel.

But among the memories which, in passing, we may recall in this old and honoured monastery, we must not omit the wonderful figure of Stephania, the widow of Crescentius, magnificent in her beauty, and terrible in her revenge, who flashes across the scene, captivates the heart of Otho, slays him in her fury at the defeat of her ambition, and vanishes out of history from that moment. According to some writers, especially of Henrion, her revenge was not satiated even by the death of Otho, but struck also at Gerbert himself, whom, at least, she was suspected of having poisoned. In this, however, there seems to be little ground of belief.[1]

[1] Otho is said by the greater part of the chroniclers of his time to have met his death in Paterno—"oppidum quod nuncupatur Paternum non longe a civitate quæ dicitur Castellana,"

G

As Paterno was much lower, and the temperature far milder than that of Vallombrosa, the monks were in the habit of passing the colder winter months here, and returning on the approach of spring to Vallombrosa. This ancient custom is still kept up by the professors, and students, and others attached to the Forestal School, by which the monastery is now occupied.

All the forests of Vallombrosa, as well as the farms and vineyards both, there and at Paterno, were most admirably planted and cultivated by the monks. In the opinion of M. Adolfo de Bérenger—and no one is more capable of giving a competent judgment on this subject, to which

says Leo Ostiensis. So also Cosimo della Rena ; but he thinks Paterno is situated about a day's journey from Todi, in the Contado di Perugia. There is no place of that name at present near Perugia, Todi, or Civita Castellana ; and for many reasons it seems most probable that it was here at this Paterno, near Tosi and Pelago, that he performed his penances, and finally was poisoned.

he has given a careful study—their forests were
" modelle de coltura forestale, perche tutti pian-
tati ad arte per filari e d'una produttività e ren-
dita giunta al di là d'ogni credere, quantunque
radicate sopra falde ertissime ed in un suolo
dirupatissimo e Sassoso." Soldani also, in his
' Guida storica per il viaggio alla Valleombrosa,'
comparing the condition of the priests in other
parts of Italy with those of Vallombrosa, points
to the latter as examples of admirable cultivation, worthy to be followed ; and after urging
upon the Government the necessity of preserv-
ing the forests of Italy from the ruin and destruction to which they were elsewhere exposed,
says,—" I shall never rest content until I see
the preservation of the forests taken in hand by
the supreme power of the Government. Among
the means which, in my opinion, are most sure
to preserve the forests on the high mountains,
are those certainly which I know by experience
to have been used in the province of Casentino

by the three monasteries of Vallombrosa, Alvernia, and Camaldoli."

As cultivators of the land, monastic bodies especially distinguished themselves, and during the middle ages they did as good service to agriculture as to literature and science. "We owe," says Hallam ('Middle Ages,' vol. iii. p. 361), "the agricultural restoration of great part of Europe to the monks. They chose, for the sake of retirement, secluded regions, which they cultivated with the labour of their hands. Many of the grants to monasteries, which strike us as enormous, were of districts absolutely wasted, which would probably have been reclaimed by no other means." Both Hallam and Guizot agree that it was the glory of St Benedict's reform that he substituted bodily labour for the supine indolence of oriental asceticism. "The Benedictines," says Guizot, "have been the great clearers of land in Europe;" "as missionaries and labourers they accomplished

their double service through peril and fatigue."
Nor were the Benedictines at Vallombrosa
exceptions to the rule.   It is to them we
owe the plantation and cultivation of all these
magnificent forests, and the admirable farming
of all this tract of country.

The Government has now possessed itself of
these forests ; and the monastery itself has been
turned into a " Collegio Forestale," professedly
for the education of young men in matters relating to agriculture.   There are thirteen professors, and only twelve scholars, in this large
building.   It is presided over by a director,
an excellent and intelligent man, who has his
suite of apartments, and lives here during the
warm seasons.   In the winter neither he nor
the professors nor scholars remain ; and the
building is occupied by three priests, also excellent men, and a few subsidiaries, whose amuse-
ment it seems to be to taunt the priests with

the loss of the monastery, and the change that liberty and unity have brought to them. Padre Furio showed us over all the building with great kindness; and, when I ventured to express my surprise at certain things, thrust out his lips and put his forefinger across them, to intimate that I might by any criticism compromise him as well as myself. So I kept silence.

Upon the establishment of the Forestal School at Vallombrosa, Signor de Bérenger was appointed director—and to no fitter hands could this office have been intrusted. During his short rule his administration of the woods was admirable. But he was not supported by the Government, and the administration has now passed into other hands. This is greatly to be regretted. Where the fault is I cannot say, but the fact is clear that little interest is shown in the matter; and the cultivation and maintenance of the forests, as well as the establishment of proper nurseries or replantation, is not what it should be, and not as it was in the time of the monks.[1] As far as is apparent, no advantage has been derived to any one by the violent sequestration and assumption of this property by the Government.

The church is not handsome architecturally, and there are few objects of interest now remaining. From a priestly point of view, the most interesting is an elaborately carved and chiselled reliquary in silver, adorned with gems, and containing the relics of San Giovanni Gualberto. In it is a brown bone, of about a foot in length, which is looked upon with reverence, and kept with great care. I do not know whether it works miracles, and I did not care to ask.

[1] M. de Bérenger has written an admirable and practical little book, entitled ' Guida per Il coltivatore dei Vivai Boschivi,' to which the reader who is interested in the question is referred.

Among the pictures which were taken from
the church, Fontani specially mentions the
celebrated picture by Pietro Perugino, now in
the academy at Florence, which formerly stood
in the choir. There still remains an Assumption by Franceschini, and a much injured Sab-
batelli in the sacristy. The cupola is painted
by Fabbrini.

There is a grand old kitchen which interested
me more, and in which there were savoury
odours, showing that whatever else is lost, the
art of cooking is not. Here in the centre is a
large circular sort of hypæthral temple—I know
not what else to call it—with stone pillars and
roof, from the centre of which hangs a turnspit,
carried by water-power, on which an ox might
be roasted whole,—a temple once dedicated to
the Genius of Hospitality and Charity, where
culinary service is still performed, though on a
much smaller scale, and where, though the
hierophants are not monks or priests, the odours

of sacrifice still rise gratefully. There is also a fine old refectory (a refectory no longer), where the brothers used to take their meals, with its reading - desk or pulpit midway on the wall above. Here, with a shudder, said Padre Furio, a ball was given a short time ago.

But change has come over almost everything. The cells of the monks are now the rooms for the students and professors. The chapel is the fencing-school. The pictures of saints on the walls have given place to crossed swords and foils. It is the epoch of equal rights (except for monks and nuns) and of union (God save the mark ! with all the old jealousies and rivalries as alive as ever, and an *octroi* at the gate of every city); of constitutional government (with almost unendurable taxation); of popular representation (the representatives agreeing in nothing but the selfish advantage of each member); of liberty (with party strife and struggle for power, and industry vainly struggling under the weight of imposts).

So let us shout " *Viva la Libertà e l'Unità!* "
while the people only shrug their shoulders and
cry "*Pazienza!*" as burden after burden is laid on
them. Words are great powers. One knows a
people by its watch-words. I am tired of hear-
ing in Italy that cry of slaves, "*Pazienza!*"
I am waiting to hear that cry of freemen—
" *Coraggio—avanti!* "

But a truce to politics. Whatever change
has taken place here at Vallombrosa, nature is
still the same. There is the vast panorama of
hills and valleys just as it was when Milton
gazed upon it—ay, just as it was when San
Giovanni Gualberto toiled with weary steps up
those wooded slopes. The same torrent and
fountain that cooled his parched lips may now
cool ours; the same deep shadows lurk under
the sombre firs; autumn still strews the sward
and heaps the brooks with the same wealth of
golden leaves torn from the chestnuts; the same

flowers smile up to us from the grass; the same tender blue sky bends over us like a benediction; and, in despite all changes and in defiance of all politics, we still can have our hour of peace and meditation and delight——" the world forgetting, by the world forgot "——along the lovely slopes of Vallombrosa.

PRINTED BY WILLIAM BLACKWOOD AND SONS.

CATALOGUE

OF

MESSRS BLACKWOOD & SONS'

PUBLICATIONS.

PHILOSOPHICAL CLASSICS FOR ENGLISH READERS.

EDITED BY WILLIAM KNIGHT, LL.D.,

Professor of Moral Philosophy in the University of St Andrews.

In crown 8vo Volumes, with Portraits, price 3s. 6d.

NOW READY.

I. **Descartes.** By Professor MAHAFFY, Dublin.

II. **Butler.** By Rev. W. L. COLLINS, M.A.

III. **Berkeley.** By Professor FRASER, Edinburgh.

The Volumes in preparation are—

IV. FICHTE. By Prof. Adamson, Owen's College, Manchester. [*Immediately.*]

HAMILTON. By Professor Veitch, Glasgow.

HUME. By the Editor.

BACON. By Professor Nichol, Glasgow.

HEGEL. By Professor Edward Caird, Glasgow.

HOBBES. By Professor Croom Robertson, London.

KANT. By William Wallace, Merton College, Oxford.

SPINOZA. By Dr Martineau, Principal of Manchester New College.

VICO. By Professor Flint, Edinburgh.

IN COURSE OF PUBLICATION.

FOREIGN CLASSICS FOR ENGLISH READERS.

EDITED BY MRS OLIPHANT.

In Crown 8vo, 2s. 6d.

The Volumes published are—

DANTE. By the Editor.

VOLTAIRE. By Major-General Sir E. B. Hamley, K.C.M.G.

PASCAL. By Principal Tulloch.

PETRARCH. By Henry Reeve, C.B.

GOETHE. By A. Hayward, Q.C.

MOLIÈRE. By the Editor and F. Tarver, M.A.

MONTAIGNE. By Rev. W. Lucas Collins, M.A.

RABELAIS. By Walter Besant, M.A.

CALDERON. By E. J. Hasell.

SAINT SIMON. By Clifton W. Collins, M.A.

CERVANTES. By the Editor.

CORNEILLE AND RACINE. By Henry M. Trollope.

In preparation—

MADAME DE SÉVIGNÉ. By Miss Thackeray.—SCHILLER. By James Sime, Author of 'Life of Lessing.'—ROUSSEAU. By Henry Graham.—LA FONTAINE. By Rev. W. Lucas Collins, M.A.

NOW COMPLETE.

ANCIENT CLASSICS FOR ENGLISH READERS.

EDITED BY THE REV. W. LUCAS COLLINS, M.A.

Complete in 28 Vols. crown 8vo, cloth, price 2s. 6d. each. And may also be had in 14 Volumes, strongly and neatly bound, with calf or vellum back, £3, 10s.

Saturday Review.—"It is difficult to estimate too highly the value of such a series as this in giving 'English readers' an insight, exact as far as it goes, into those olden times which are so remote and yet to many of us so close."

CATALOGUE

OF

MESSRS BLACKWOOD & SONS'

PUBLICATIONS.

———◆———

ALISON. History of Europe. By Sir Archibald Alison, Bart., D.C.L.

1. From the Commencement of the French Revolution to the Battle of Waterloo.
   Library Edition, 14 vols., with Portraits. Demy 8vo, £10, 10s.
   Another Edition, in 20 vols. crown 8vo, £6.
   People's Edition, 13 vols. crown 8vo, £2, 11s.

2. Continuation to the Accession of Louis Napoleon.
   Library Edition, 8 vols. 8vo, £6, 7s. 6d.
   People's Edition, 8 vols. crown 8vo, 34s.

3. Epitome of Alison's History of Europe. Twenty-eighth Thousand, 7s. 6d.

4. Atlas to Alison's History of Europe. By A. Keith Johnston.
   Library Edition, demy 4to, £3, 3s.
   People's Edition, 31s. 6d.

———— Life of John Duke of Marlborough. With some Account of his Contemporaries, and of the War of the Succession. Third Edition, 2 vols. 8vo. Portraits and Maps, 30s.

———— Essays : Historical, Political, and Miscellaneous. 3 vols. demy 8vo, 45s.

———— Lives of Lord Castlereagh and Sir Charles Stewart, Second and Third Marquesses of Londonderry. From the Original Papers of the Family. 3 vols. 8vo, £2, 2s.

———— Principles of the Criminal Law of Scotland. 8vo, 18s.

———— Practice of the Criminal Law of Scotland. 8vo, cloth boards, 18s.

———— The Principles of Population, and their Connection with Human Happiness. 2 vols. 8vo, 30s.

ALISON. On the Management of the Poor in Scotland, and its Effects on the Health of the Great Towns. By William Pulteney Alison, M.D. Crown 8vo, 5s. 6d.

ADAMS. Great Campaigns. A Succinct Account of the Principal Military Operations which have taken place in Europe from 1796 to 1870. By Major C. Adams, Professor of Military History at the Staff College. Edited by Captain C. Cooper King, R.M. Artillery, Instructor of Tactics, Royal Military College. 8vo, with Maps. 16s.

AIRD. Poetical Works of Thomas Aird. Fifth Edition, with Memoir of the Author by the Rev. JARDINE WALLACE, and Portrait. Crown 8vo, 7s. 6d.

———— The Old Bachelor in the Old Scottish Village. Fcap. 8vo, 4s.

ALEXANDER. Moral Causation ; or, Notes on Mr Mill's Notes to the Chapter on "Freedom" in the Third Edition of his 'Examination of Sir William Hamilton's Philosophy.' By PATRICK PROCTOR ALEXANDER, M.A., Author of 'Mill and Carlyle,' &c. Second Edition, revised and extended. Crown 8vo, 6s.

ALLARDYCE. The City of Sunshine. By ALEXANDER ALLARDYCE. Three vols. post 8vo, £1, 5s. 6d.

ANCIENT CLASSICS FOR ENGLISH READERS. Edited by Rev. W. LUCAS COLLINS, M.A. Complete in 28 vols., cloth, 2s. 6d. each ; or in 14 vols., tastefully bound with calf or vellum back, £3, 10s.

Contents of the Series.

HOMER: THE ILIAD. By the Editor.
HOMER: THE ODYSSEY. By the Editor.
HERODOTUS. By George C. Swayne, M.A.
XENOPHON. By Sir Alexander Grant, Bart., LL.D.
EURIPIDES. By W. B. Donne.
ARISTOPHANES. By the Editor.
PLATO. By Clifton W. Collins, M.A.
LUCIAN. By the Editor.
ÆSCHYLUS. By the Right Rev. the Bishop of Colombo.
SOPHOCLES. By Clifton W. Collins, M.A.
HESIOD AND THEOGNIS. By the Rev. J. Davies, M.A.
GREEK ANTHOLOGY. By Lord Neaves.
VIRGIL. By the Editor.
HORACE. By Sir Theodore Martin, K.C.B.
JUVENAL. By Edward Walford, M.A.

PLAUTUS AND TERENCE. By the Editor.
THE COMMENTARIES OF CÆSAR. By Anthony Trollope.
TACITUS. By W. B. Donne.
CICERO. By the Editor.
PLINY'S LETTERS. By the Rev. Alfred Church, M.A., and the Rev. W. J. Brodribb, M.A.
LIVY. By the Editor.
OVID. By the Rev. A. Church, M.A.
CATULLUS, TIBULLUS, AND PROPERTIUS. By the Rev. Jas. Davies, M.A.
DEMOSTHENES. By the Rev. W. J. Brodribb, M.A.
ARISTOTLE. By Sir Alexander Grant, Bart., LL.D.
THUCYDIDES. By the Editor.
LUCRETIUS. By W. H. Mallock, M.A.
PINDAR. By the Rev. F. D. Morice, M.A.

AYLWARD. The Transvaal of To-day: War, Witchcraft, Sports, and Spoils in South Africa. By ALFRED AYLWARD, Commandant, Transvaal Republic ; Captain (late) Lydenberg Volunteer Corps. Second Edition. Crown 8vo, with a Map, 6s.

AYTOUN. Lays of the Scottish Cavaliers, and other Poems. By W. EDMONDSTOUNE AYTOUN, D.C.L., Professor of Rhetoric and Belles-Lettres in the University of Edinburgh. Twenty-seventh Edition. Fcap. 8vo, 7s. 6d.

———— An Illustrated Edition of the Lays of the Scottish Cavaliers. From designs by Sir NOEL PATON. Small 4to, 21s., in gilt cloth.

———— Bothwell : a Poem. Third Edition. Fcap., 7s. 6d.

———— Firmilian ; or, The Student of Badajoz. A Spasmodic Tragedy. Fcap., 5s.

———— Poems and Ballads of Goethe. Translated by Professor AYTOUN and Sir THEODORE MARTIN, K.C.B. Third Edition. Fcap., 6s.

———— Bon Gaultier's Book of Ballads. By the SAME. Thirteenth Edition. With Illustrations by Doyle, Leech, and Crowquill. Post 8vo, gilt edges, 8s. 6d.

———— The Ballads of Scotland. Edited by Professor AYTOUN. Fourth Edition. 2 vols. fcap. 8vo, 12s.

———— Memoir of William E. Aytoun, D.C.L. By Sir THEODORE MARTIN, K.C.B. With Portrait. Post 8vo, 12s.

BAGOT. The Art of Poetry of Horace. Free and Explanatory Translations in Prose and Verse. By the Very Rev. DANIEL BAGOT, D.D. Third Edition, Revised, printed on papier vergé, square 8vo, 5s.

BAIRD LECTURES. The Mysteries of Christianity. By T. J. CRAWFORD, D.D., F.R.S.E., Professor of Divinity in the University of Edinburgh, &c. Being the Baird Lecture for 1874. Crown 8vo, 7s. 6d.

———— Endowed Territorial Work : Its Supreme Importance to the Church and Country. By WILLIAM SMITH, D.D., Minister of North Leith. Being the Baird Lecture for 1875. Crown 8vo, 6s.

———— Theism. By ROBERT FLINT, D.D., LL.D., Professor of Divinity in the University of Edinburgh. Being the Baird Lecture for 1876. Third Edition. Crown 8vo, 7s. 6d.

———— Anti-Theistic Theories. By the SAME. Being the Baird Lecture for 1877. Second Edition. Crown 8vo, 10s. 6d.

BATTLE OF DORKING. Reminiscences of a Volunteer. From 'Blackwood's Magazine.' Second Hundredth Thousand. 6d.

BY THE SAME AUTHOR.

The Dilemma. Cheap Edition. Crown 8vo, 6s.

A True Reformer. 3 vols. crown 8vo, £1, 5s. 6d.

BESANT. Readings from Rabelais. By WALTER BESANT, M.A. In one volume, post 8vo. [In the press.

BLACKIE. Lays and Legends of Ancient Greece. By JOHN STUART BLACKIE, Professor of Greek in the University of Edinburgh. Second Edition. Fcap. 8vo. 5s.

BLACKWOOD'S MAGAZINE, from Commencement in 1817 to June 1880. Nos. 1 to 776, forming 127 Volumes.

———— Index to Blackwood's Magazine. Vols. 1 to 50. 8vo, 15s.

———— Tales from Blackwood. Forming Twelve Volumes of Interesting and Amusing Railway Reading. Price One Shilling each in Paper Cover. Sold separately at all Railway Bookstalls.

They may also be had bound in cloth, 18s., and in half calf, richly gilt, 30s. or 12 volumes in 6, half Roxburghe, 21s., and half red morocco, 28s.

———— Tales from Blackwood. New Series. Complete in Twenty-four Shilling Parts. Handsomely bound in 12 vols., cloth, 30s. In leather back, Roxburghe style, 37s. 6d. In half calf, gilt, 52s. 6d. In half morocco, 55s.

———— Standard Novels. Uniform in size and legibly Printed. Each Novel complete in one volume.

Florin Series, Illustrated Boards.

TOM CRINGLE'S LOG. By Michael Scott.	PEN OWEN. By Dean Hook.
THE CRUISE OF THE MIDGE. By the Same.	ADAM BLAIR. By J. G. Lockhart.
CYRIL THORNTON. By Captain Hamilton.	LADY LEE'S WIDOWHOOD. By General
ANNALS OF THE PARISH. By John Galt.	Sir E. B. Hamley.
THE PROVOST, &c. By John Galt.	SALEM CHAPEL. By Mrs Oliphant.
SIR ANDREW WYLIE. By John Galt.	THE PERPETUAL CURATE. By Mrs Oli-
THE ENTAIL. By John Galt.	phant.
MISS MOLLY. By Beatrice May Butt.	MISS MARJORIBANKS. By Mrs Oliphant.
REGINALD DALTON. By J. G. Lockhart.	JOHN : A Love Story. By Mrs Oliphant.

Or in Cloth Boards, 2s. 6d.

Shilling Series, Illustrated Cover.

THE RECTOR, and THE DOCTOR'S FAMILY. By Mrs Oliphant.	SIR FRIZZLE PUMPKIN, NIGHTS AT MESS, &c.
THE LIFE OF MANSIE WAUCH. By D. M. Moir.	THE SUBALTERN.
	LIFE IN THE FAR WEST. By G. F. Ruxton.
PENINSULAR SCENES AND SKETCHES. By F. Hardman.	VALERIUS : A Roman Story. By J. G. Lockhart.

Or in Cloth Boards, 1s. 6d.

BLACKMORE. The Maid of Sker. By R. D. BLACKMORE, Author of 'Lorna Doone,' &c. Seventh Edition. Crown 8vo, 7s. 6d.

BOSCOBEL TRACTS. Relating to the Escape of Charles the Second after the Battle of Worcester, and his subsequent Adventures. Edited by J Hughes, Esq., A.M. A New Edition, with additional Notes and Illustrations, including Communications from the Rev. R. H. Barham, Author of the 'Ingoldsby Legends.' 8vo, with Engravings, 16s.

BRACKENBURY. A Narrative of the Ashanti War. Prepared from the official documents, by permission of Major-General Sir Garnet Wolseley, K.C.B., K.C.M.G. By Major H. Brackenbury, R.A., Assistant Military Secretary to Sir Garnet Wolseley. With Maps from the latest Surveys made by the Staff of the Expedition. 2 vols. 8vo, 25s.

BROOKE, Life of Sir James, Rajah of Sarāwak. From his Personal Papers and Correspondence. By Spenser St John, H.M.'s Minister-Resident and Consul-General Peruvian Republic; formerly Secretary to the Rajah. With Portrait and a Map. Post 8vo, 12s. 6d.

BROUGHAM. Memoirs of the Life and Times of Henry Lord Brougham. Written by Himself. 3 vols. 8vo, £2, 8s. The Volumes are sold separately, price 16s. each.

BROWN. The Forester: A Practical Treatise on the Planting, Rearing, and General Management of Forest-trees. By James Brown, Wood-Surveyor and Nurseryman. Fifth Edition, revised and enlarged. Royal 8vo, with Engravings. [In the press.

BROWN. The Ethics of George Eliot's Works. By John Crombie Brown. Third Edition. Crown 8vo, 2s. 6d.

BROWN. A Manual of Botany, Anatomical and Physiological. For the Use of Students. By Robert Brown, M.A., Ph.D., F.L.S., F.R.G.S. Crown 8vo, with numerous Illustrations, 12s. 6d.

BROWN. Book of the Landed Estate. Containing Directions for the Management and Development of the Resources of Landed Property. By Robert E. Brown, Factor and Estate Agent. Large 8vo, with Illustrations, 21s.

BUCHAN. Introductory Text-Book of Meteorology. By Alexander Buchan, M.A., F.R.S.E., Secretary of the Scottish Meteorological Society, &c. Crown 8vo, with 8 Coloured Charts and other Engravings, pp. 218. 4s. 6d.

BURBIDGE. Domestic Floriculture, Window Gardening, and Floral Decorations. Being practical directions for the Propagation, Culture, and Arrangement of Plants and Flowers as Domestic Ornaments. By F. W. Burbidge. Second Edition. Crown 8vo, with numerous Illustrations, 7s. 6d.

———— Cultivated Plants: Their Propagation and Improvement. Including Natural and Artificial Hybridisation, Raising from Seed, Cuttings, and Layers, Grafting and Budding, as applied to the Families and Genera in Cultivation. Crown 8vo, with numerous Illustrations, 12s. 6d.

BURN. Handbook of the Mechanical Arts Concerned in the Construction and Arrangement of Dwelling-Houses and other Buildings; with Practical Hints on Road-making and the Enclosing of Land. By Robert Scott Burn, Engineer. Second Edition. Crown 8vo, 6s. 6d.

BUTE. The Roman Breviary: Reformed by Order of the Holy Œcumenical Council of Trent; Published by Order of Pope St Pius V.; and Revised by Clement VIII. and Urban VIII.; together with the Offices since granted. Translated out of Latin into English by John, Marquess of Bute, K.T. In 2 vols. crown 8vo, cloth boards, edges uncut. £2, 2s.

BUTT. Miss Molly. By Beatrice May Butt. Cheap Edition, 2s.

———— Delicia. By the Author of 'Miss Molly.' Fourth Edition. Crown 8vo, 7s. 6d.

BURTON. The History of Scotland: From Agricola's Invasion to the Extinction of the last Jacobite Insurrection. By John Hill Burton, D.C.L., Historiographer-Royal for Scotland. New and Enlarged Edition, 8 vols., and Index. Crown 8vo, £3, 3s.

BURTON. History of the British Empire during the Reign of Queen Anne. In 3 vols. 8vo. 36s.

——— The Cairngorm Mountains. Crown 8vo, 3s. 6d.

CAIRD. Sermons. By JOHN CAIRD, D.D., Principal of the University of Glasgow. Fourteenth Thousand. Fcap. 8vo, 5s.

——— Religion in Common Life. A Sermon preached in Crathie Church, October 14, 1855, before Her Majesty the Queen and Prince Albert. Published by Her Majesty's Command. Price One Shilling. Cheap Edition, 3d.

CAMPBELL, Life of Colin, Lord Clyde. See General SHADWELL, at page 20.

CARLYLE. Autobiography of the Rev. Dr Alexander Carlyle, Minister of Inveresk. Containing Memorials of the Men and Events of his Time. Edited by JOHN HILL BURTON. 8vo. Third Edition, with Portrait, 14s.

CAUVIN. A Treasury of the English and German Languages. Compiled from the best Authors and Lexicographers in both Languages. Adapted to the Use of Schools, Students, Travellers, and Men of Business; and forming a Companion to all German-English Dictionaries. By JOSEPH CAUVIN, LL.D. & Ph.D., of the University of Göttingen, &c. Crown 8vo, 7s. 6d.

CHARTERIS. Canonicity; or, Early Testimonies to the Existence and Use of the Books of the New Testament. Based on Kirchhoffer's 'Quellensammlung.' Edited by A. H. CHARTERIS, D.D., Professor of Biblical Criticism in the University of Edinburgh. 8vo, 18s.

——— Life of the Rev. James Robertson, D.D., F.R.S.E., Professor of Divinity and Ecclesiastical History in the University of Edinburgh. By Professor CHARTERIS. With Portrait. 8vo, 10s. 6d.

CHETWYND. Life in a German Village. By the Hon. Mrs HENRY WEYLAND CHETWYND, Author of 'Neighbours and Friends,' 'Janie, 'Mdlle. d'Estanville,' &c. &c. Second Edition. Crown 8vo, 7s. 6d.

CHEVELEY NOVELS, THE.
I. A MODERN MINISTER. 2 vols. bound in cloth, with Twenty-six Illustrations. 17s.
II. SAUL WEIR. 2 vols. bound in cloth. With Twelve Illustrations by F. Barnard. 16s.

CHIROL. 'Twixt Greek and Turk. By M. VALENTINE CHIROL. In one volume, post 8vo. With Frontispiece and Map. [In the press.

CHURCH SERVICE SOCIETY. A Book of Common Order: Being Forms of Worship issued by the Church Service Society. Fourth Edition, 5s.

COLQUHOUN. The Moor and the Loch. Containing Minute Instructions in all Highland Sports, with Wanderings over Crag and Corrie, Flood and Fell. By JOHN COLQUHOUN. Fifth Edition, greatly enlarged. With Illustrations. 2 vols. post 8vo, 26s.

COTTERILL. The Genesis of the Church. By the Right. Rev. HENRY COTTERILL, D.D., Bishop of Edinburgh. Demy 8vo, 16s.

CRANSTOUN. The Elegies of Albius Tibullus. Translated into English Verse, with Life of the Poet, and Illustrative Notes. By JAMES CRANSTOUN, LL.D., Author of a Translation of 'Catullus.' Crown 8vo, 6s. 6d.

——— The Elegies of Sextus Propertius. Translated into English Verse, with Life of the Poet, and Illustrative Notes. Crown 8vo, 7s. 6d.

CRAWFORD. The Doctrine of Holy Scripture respecting the Atonement. By the late THOMAS J. CRAWFORD, D.D., Professor of Divinity in the University of Edinburgh. Third Edition. 8vo, 12s.

CRAWFORD. The Fatherhood of God, Considered in its General and Special Aspects, and particularly in relation to the Atonement, with a Review of Recent Speculations on the Subject. Third Edition, Revised and Enlarged. 8vo, 9s.

———— The Preaching of the Cross, and other Sermons. 8vo, 7s. 6d.

———— The Mysteries of Christianity; being the Baird Lecture for 1874. Crown 8vo, 7s. 6d.

CROSSE. Round about the Carpathians. By ANDREW F. CROSSE, F.C.S. 8vo, with Map of the Author's route, price 12s. 6d.

DESCARTES. The Method, Meditations, and Principles of Philosophy of Descartes. Translated from the Original French and Latin. With a New Introductory Essay, Historical and Critical, on the Cartesian Philosophy. By JOHN VEITCH, LL.D., Professor of Logic and Rhetoric in the University of Glasgow. A New Edition, being the Eighth. Price 6s. 6d.

DICKSON. Japan; being a Sketch of the History, Government, and Officers of the Empire. By WALTER DICKSON. 8vo, 15s.

DU CANE. The Odyssey of Homer, Books I.-XII. Translated into English Verse. By Sir CHARLES DU CANE, K.C.M.G. 8vo, 10s. 6d.

EAGLES. Essays. By the Rev. JOHN EAGLES, A.M. Oxon. Originally published in 'Blackwood's Magazine.' Post 8vo, 10s. 6d.

———— The Sketcher. Originally published in 'Blackwood's Magazine.' Post 8vo, 10s. 6d.

ELIOT. Impressions of Theophrastus Such. By GEORGE ELIOT. Fourth Edition. Post 8vo, 10s. 6d. New and cheaper Edition. Crown 8vo, 5s.

———— Adam Bede. Illustrated Edition. 3s. 6d., cloth.

———— The Mill on the Floss. Illustrated Edition. 3s. 6d., cloth.

———— Scenes of Clerical Life. Illustrated Edition. 3s., cloth.

———— Silas Marner: The Weaver of Raveloe. Illustrated Edition. 2s. 6d., cloth.

———— Felix Holt, the Radical. Illustrated Edition. 3s. 6d., cloth.

———— Romola. With Vignette. 3s. 6d., cloth.

———— Middlemarch. Crown 8vo, 7s. 6d.

———— Daniel Deronda. Crown 8vo, 7s. 6d.

———— Works of George Eliot (Cabinet Edition). Complete and Uniform Edition, handsomely printed in a new type, 20 volumes, crown 8vo price £5. The Volumes are also sold separately, price 5s. each, viz.:—
Romola. 2 vols.—Silas Marner, The Lifted Veil, Brother Jacob. 1 vol.—Adam Bede. 2 vols.—Scenes of Clerical Life. 2 vols.—The Mill on the Floss. 2 vols.—Felix Holt. 2 vols.—Middlemarch. 3 vols.—Daniel Deronda. 3 vols —The Spanish Gypsy. 1 vol.—Jubal, and other Poems, Old and New. 1 vol.—Theophrastus Such. 1 vol.

———— The Spanish Gypsy. Seventh Edition. Crown 8vo, 7s. 6d., cloth.

———— The Legend of Jubal, and other Poems. New Edition. Fcap. 8vo, 5s., cloth.

———— Wise, Witty, and Tender Sayings, in Prose and Verse. Selected from the Works of GEORGE ELIOT. Fifth Edition. Fcap. 8vo, 6s.

———— The George Eliot Birthday Book. Printed on fine paper, with red border, and handsomely bound in cloth, gilt. Fcap. 8vo, cloth, 3s. 6d. And in French morocco or Russia, 5s.

ESSAYS ON SOCIAL SUBJECTS. Originally published in the 'Saturday Review.' A New Edition. **First** and Second Series. 2 vols. crown 8vo, 6s. each.

EWALD. The **Crown** and its Advisers ; **or,** Queen, Ministers, Lords, and Commons. By ALEXANDER **CHARLES EWALD,** F.S.A. Crown 8vo, 5s.

FERRIER. Philosophical Works of the late James **F.** Ferrier, **B.A.** Oxon., Professor of Moral Philosophy and Political Economy, St Andrews. New Edition. Edited by Sir ALEX. GRANT, Bart., D.C.L., and Professor LUSHINGTON. 3 vols. crown 8vo, 34s. 6d.

——— Institutes of Metaphysic. Third **Edition. 10s. 6d.**

——— Lectures on the **Early** Greek Philosophy. Third **Edition.** 10s. 6d.

——— Philosophical **Remains, including** the Lectures **on Early** Greek Philosophy. 2 vols., 24s.

FERRIER. George Eliot and **Judaism. An** Attempt to appreciate ' Daniel Deronda.' By Professor DAVID KAUFMANN, of the Jewish Theological Seminary, Buda-Pesth. Translated from the German by J. W. FERRIER. Second Edition. Crown 8vo, 2s. 6d.

FINLAY. History **of Greece under** Foreign **Domination. By** the late GEORGE FINLAY, LL.D., Athens. 6 vols. 8vo—viz. :

Greece under the Romans. B.C. 146 to A.D. 717. A Historical View of the Condition of the Greek Nation from its Conquest by the Romans until the Extinction of the Roman Power in the East. Second Edition, 16s.

History of the Byzantine Empire. A.D. **716 to 1204 ;** and of the Greek Empire of Nicæa and Constantinople, **A.D. 1204 to 1453.** 2 vols., £1, 7s. 6d.

Greece under Othoman and Venetian Domination. A.D. 1453 to 1821. 10s. 6d.

History of the Greek Revolution of 1830. 2 vols. 8vo, £1, 4s.

FLINT. **The** Philosophy of History in Europe. Vol. I., containing the History of that Philosophy in France and Germany. By ROBERT FLINT, D.D., LL.D., Professor of Divinity, University of Edinburgh. 8vo, 15s.

——— Theism. **Being the Baird** Lecture for 1876. Third **Edition.** Crown 8vo, 7s. 6d.

——— Anti-Theistic Theories. Being the Baird **Lecture for 1877.** Second Edition. Crown 8vo, 10s. 6d.

FORBES. The Campaign of Garibaldi in the Two Sicilies : **A Per-**sonal Narrative. By CHARLES STUART FORBES, Commander, R.N. **Post 8vo,** with Portraits, 12s.

FOREIGN CLASSICS FOR ENGLISH **READERS. Edited** by Mrs OLIPHANT. Price 2s. 6d.

Now published :—I. DANTE. By the Editor.—II. VOLTAIRE. By Major-General Sir E. B. Hamley.—III. PASCAL. By Principal Tulloch.—IV. PETRARCH. By Henry Reeve, C.B.—V. GOETHE. By A. Hayward, Q.C.—VI. MOLIÈRE. By the Editor and F. Tarver, M.A.—VII. MONTAIGNE. By Rev. W. L. Collins, M.A.—VIII. RABELAIS. By Walter Besant, M.A.—IX. CALDERON. By E. **J.** Hasell.—X. SAINT SIMON. By Clifton W. Collins, M.A.—XI. CERVANTES. By the Editor.—XII CORNEILLE AND RACINE. By Henry M. Trollope.

In preparation :—MADAME DE SÉVIGNÉ. By Miss Thackeray.—**SCHILLER.** By James Sime, Author of ' Life of Lessing.'—ROUSSEAU. **By Henry** Graham.—LA FONTAINE. By Rev W. **L.** Collins, M.A.

FRASER. Handy Book of Ornamental Conifers, and of Rhododendrons and other American Flowering Shrubs, suitable for the Climate and Soils of Britain. With descriptions of the best kinds, and containing Useful Hints for their successful Cultivation. By HUGH FRASER, Fellow of the Botanical Society of Edinburgh. Crown 8vo, 6s.

GALT. Annals of the Parish. By JOHN GALT. Fcap. 8vo, 2s.

—— The Provost. Fcap. 8vo, 2s.

—— Sir Andrew Wylie. Fcap. 8vo, 2s.

—— The Entail; or, The Laird of Grippy. Fcap. 8vo, 2s.

GARDENER, THE: A Magazine of Horticulture and Floriculture. Edited by DAVID THOMSON, Author of 'The Handy Book of the Flower-Garden,' &c.; Assisted by a Staff of the best practical Writers. Published Monthly, 6d

GENERAL ASSEMBLY OF THE CHURCH OF SCOTLAND.

—— Family Prayers. Authorised by the General Assembly of the Church of Scotland. A New Edition, crown 8vo, in large type, 4s. 6d. Another Edition, crown 8vo, 2s.

—— Prayers for Social and Family Worship. For the Use of Soldiers, Sailors, Colonists, and Sojourners in India, and other Persons, at home and abroad, who are deprived of the ordinary services of a Christian Ministry. Cheap Edition, 1s. 6d.

—— The Scottish Hymnal. Hymns for Public Worship. Published for Use in Churches by Authority of the General Assembly. Various sizes—viz.: 1. Large type, for pulpit use, cloth, 3s. 6d. 2. Longprimer type, cloth, red edges, 1s. 6d.; French morocco, 2s. 6d.; calf, 6s. 3. Bourgeois type, cloth, red edges, 1s.; French morocco, 2s. 4. Minion type, limp cloth, 6d.; French morocco, 1s. 6d. 5. School Edition, in paper cover, 2d. 6. Children's Hymnal, paper cover, 1d. No. 2, bound with the Psalms and Paraphrases, cloth, 3s.; French morocco, 4s. 6d.; calf, 7s. 6d. No. 3, bound with the Psalms and Paraphrases, cloth, 2s.; French morocco, 3s.

—— The Scottish Hymnal, with Music. Selected by the Committees on Hymns and on Psalmody. The harmonies arranged by W. H. Monk. Cloth, 1s. 6d.; French morocco, 3s. 6d. The same in the Tonic Sol-fa Notation, 1s. 6d. and 3s. 6d.

GERARD. Reata: What's in a Name? By E. D. GERARD. New Edition. In one volume, crown 8vo. [Nearly ready.

GLEIG. The Subaltern. By G. R. GLEIG, M.A., late Chaplain-General of her Majesty's Forces. Originally published in 'Blackwood's Magazine.' Library Edition. Revised and Corrected, with a New Preface. Crown 8vo, 7s. 6d.

GOETHE'S FAUST. Translated into English Verse by Sir THEODORE MARTIN, K.C.B. Second Edition, post 8vo, 6s. Cheap Edition, fcap., 3s. 6d.

—— Poems and Ballads of Goethe. Translated by Professor AYTOUN and Sir THEODORE MARTIN, K.C.B. Third Edition, fcap. 8vo, 6s.

GORDON CUMMING. At Home in Fiji. By C. F. GORDON CUMMING, Author of 'From the Hebrides to the Himalayas.' 2 vols. 8vo. With Illustrations and Map. 25s.

GRAHAM. Annals and Correspondence of the Viscount and First and Second Earls of Stair. By JOHN MURRAY GRAHAM. 2 vols. demy 8vo, with Portraits and other Illustrations. £1, 8s.

—— Memoir of Lord Lynedoch. Second Edition, crown 8vo, 5s.

GRANT. Bush-Life in Queensland. By A. C. GRANT. In 2 vols. post 8vo.

GRANT. Incidents in the Sepoy War of 1857-58. Compiled from the Private Journals of the late General Sir HOPE GRANT, G.C.B. ; together with some Explanatory Chapters by Captain HENRY KNOLLYS, R.A. Crown 8vo, with Map and Plans, 12s.

GRANT. Memorials of the Castle of Edinburgh. By JAMES GRANT. A New Edition. Crown 8vo, with 12 Engravings, 3s.

HAMERTON. Wenderholme : A Story of Lancashire and Yorkshire Life. By PHILIP GILBERT HAMERTON, Author of 'A Painter's Camp.' A New Edition. Crown 8vo, 6s.

HAMILTON. Lectures on Metaphysics. By Sir WILLIAM HAMILTON, Bart., Professor of Logic and Metaphysics in the University of Edinburgh. Edited by the Rev. H. L. MANSEL, B.D., LL.D., Dean of St Paul's ; and JOHN VEITCH, M.A., Professor of Logic and Rhetoric, Glasgow. Sixth Edition. 2 vols. 8vo, 24s.

———— Lectures on Logic. Edited by the SAME. Third Edition. 2 vols. 24s.

———— Discussions on Philosophy and Literature, Education and University Reform. Third Edition. 8vo, 21s.

———— Memoir of Sir William Hamilton, Bart., Professor of Logic and Metaphysics in the University of Edinburgh. By Professor VEITCH of the University of Glasgow. 8vo, with Portrait, 18s.

HAMILTON. Annals of the Peninsular Campaigns. By Captain THOMAS HAMILTON. Edited by F. Hardman. 8vo, 16s. Atlas of Maps to illustrate the Campaigns, 12s.

HAMLEY. The Operations of War Explained and Illustrated. By Sir EDWARD BRUCE HAMLEY, C.B. Fourth Edition, revised throughout. 4to, with numerous Illustrations, 30s.

———— Thomas Carlyle : An Essay. Second Edition. Crown 8vo. 2s. 6d.

———— The Story of the Campaign of Sebastopol. Written in the Camp. With Illustrations drawn in Camp by the Author. 8vo, 21s.

———— On Outposts. Second Edition. 8vo, 2s.

———— Wellington's Career ; A Military and Political Summary. Crown 8vo, 2s.

———— Lady Lee's Widowhood. Crown 8vo, 2s. 6d.

———— Our Poor Relations. A Philozoic Essay. With Illustrations, chiefly by Ernest Griset. Crown 8vo, cloth gilt, 3s. 6d.

HAMLEY. Guilty, or Not Guilty ? A Tale. By Major-General W. G. HAMLEY, late of the Royal Engineers. New Edition. Crown 8vo, 3s. 6d.

———— The House of Lys : One Book of its History. A Tale. Second Edition. 2 vols. crown 8vo. 17s.

HANDY HORSE-BOOK ; or, Practical Instructions in Riding, Driving, and the General Care and Management of Horses. By 'MAGENTA.' Ninth Edition, with 6 Engravings, 4s. 6d.

BY THE SAME.

Our Domesticated Dogs : their Treatment in reference to Food, Diseases, Habits, Punishment, Accomplishments. Crown 8vo, 2s. 6d.

HARBORD. A Glossary of Navigation. Containing the Definitions and Propositions of the Science, Explanation of Terms, and Description of Instruments. By the Rev. J. B. HARBORD, M.A., Assistant Director of Education, Admiralty. Crown 8vo. Illustrated with Diagrams, 6s.

———— Definitions and Diagrams in Astronomy and Navigation. 1s.

———— Short Sermons for Hospitals and Sick Seamen. Fcap. 8vo, cloth, 4s. 6d.

HARDMAN. Scenes and Adventures in Central America. Edited by FREDERICK HARDMAN. Crown 8vo, 6s.

HAWKEY. The Shakespeare Tapestry. Woven in Verse. By C. HAWKEY. Fcap. 8vo. 6s.

HAY. The Works of the Right Rev. Dr George Hay, Bishop of Edinburgh. Edited under the Supervision of the Right Rev Bishop STRAIN. With Memoir and Portrait of the Author. 5 vols. crown 8vo, bound in extra cloth, £1, 1s. Or, sold separately—viz. :

———— The Sincere Christian Instructed in the Faith of Christ from the Written Word. 2 vols., 8s.

———— The Devout Christian Instructed in the Law of Christ from the Written Word. 2 vols., 8s.

———— The Pious Christian Instructed in the Nature and Practice of the Principal Exercises of Piety. 1 vol., 4s.

HEMANS. The Poetical Works of Mrs Hemans. Copyright Editions.

One Volume, royal 8vo, 5s.

The Same, with Illustrations engraved on Steel, bound in cloth, gilt edges, 7s. 6d.

Six Volumes, fcap., 12s. 6d.

Seven Volumes, fcap., with Memoir by her SISTER. 35s.

SELECT POEMS OF MRS HEMANS. Fcap., cloth, gilt edges, 3s.

———— Memoir of Mrs Hemans. By her SISTER. With a Portrait, fcap. 8vo, 5s.

HOLE. A Book about Roses: How to Grow and Show Them. By the Rev Canon HOLE. With coloured Frontispiece by the Hon. Mrs Francklin. Seventh Edition, revised. Crown 8vo, 7s. 6d.

HOME PRAYERS. By Ministers of the Church of Scotland and Members of the Church Service Society. Fcap. 8vo, price 3s.

HOMER. The Odyssey. Translated into English Verse in the Spenserian Stanza. By PHILIP STANHOPE WORSLEY. Third Edition, 2 vols., fcap., 12s.

———— The Iliad. Translated by P. S. WORSLEY and Professor CONINGTON. 2 vols. crown 8vo, 21s.

HOSACK. Mary Queen of Scots and Her Accusers. Containing a Variety of Documents never before published. By JOHN HOSACK, Barrister-at-Law. A New and Enlarged Edition, with a Photograph from the Bust on the Tomb in Westminster Abbey. 2 vols. 8vo, £1, 1s.

INDEX GEOGRAPHICUS : Being a List, alphabetically arranged, of the Principal Places on the Globe, with the Countries and Subdivisions of the Countries in which they are situated, and their Latitudes and Longitudes. Applicable to all Modern Atlases and Maps. Imperial 8vo, pp. 676, 21s.

JEAN JAMBON. Our Trip to Blunderland ; or, Grand Excursion to Blundertown and Back. By JEAN JAMBON. With Sixty Illustrations designed by CHARLES DOYLE, engraved by DALZIEL. Fourth Thousand. Handsomely bound in cloth, gilt edges, 6s. 6d. Cheap Edition, cloth, 3s. 6d. In boards, 2s. 6d.

JOHNSON. The Scots Musical Museum. Consisting of upwards of Six Hundred Songs, with proper Basses for the Pianoforte. Originally published by JAMES JOHNSON ; and now accompanied with Copious Notes and Illustrations of the Lyric Poetry and Music of Scotland, by the late WILLIAM STENHOUSE ; with additional Notes and Illustrations, by DAVID LAING and C. K. SHARPE. 4 vols. 8vo, Roxburghe binding, £2, 12s. 6d.

JOHNSTON. The Chemistry of Common Life. By Professor J. F. W. JOHNSTON. New Edition, Revised, and brought down to date. By ARTHUR HERBERT CHURCH, M.A. Oxon. ; Author of 'Food: its Sources, Constituents, and Uses;' 'The Laboratory Guide for Agricultural Students;' 'Plain Words about Water,' &c. Illustrated with Maps and 102 Engravings on Wood. Complete in One Volume, crown 8vo, pp. 618, 7s. 6d.

———— Professor Johnston's Elements of Agricultural Chemistry and Geology. Twelfth Edition, Revised, and brought down to date. By CHARLES A. CAMERON, M.D., F.R.C.S.I., &c. Fcap. 8vo, 6s. 6d.

———— Catechism of Agricultural Chemistry and Geology. An entirely New Edition, revised and enlarged, by CHARLES A. CAMERON, M.D., F.R.C.S.I., &c. Seventy-eighth Thousand, with numerous Illustrations, 1s.

———— Notes on North America: Agricultural, Economical, and Social. 2 vols. post 8vo, 21s.

KING. The Metamorphoses of Ovid. Translated in English Blank Verse. By HENRY KING, M.A., Fellow of Wadham College, Oxford, and of the Inner Temple, Barrister-at-Law. Crown 8vo, 10s. 6d.

KINGLAKE. History of the Invasion of the Crimea. By A. W. KINGLAKE. Cabinet Edition. **Six Volumes, crown 8vo, at 6s. each.** The Volumes respectively contain :—

    I. THE ORIGIN OF THE WAR between the Czar and the Sultan.
    II. RUSSIA MET AND INVADED. With 4 Maps and Plans.
    III. THE BATTLE OF THE ALMA. With 14 Maps and Plans.
    IV. SEBASTOPOL AT BAY. With 10 Maps and Plans.
    V. THE BATTLE OF BALACLAVA. With 10 Maps and Plans.
    VI. THE BATTLE OF INKERMAN. With 11 Maps and Plans.

———— History of the Invasion of the Crimea. Vol. VI. Winter Troubles. Demy 8vo, with a Map, 16s.

———— Eothen. A New Edition, uniform with the Cabinet Edition of the 'History of the Crimean War,' price 6s.

KNOLLYS. The Elements of Field-Artillery. Designed for the Use of Infantry and Cavalry Officers. By HENRY KNOLLYS, Captain Royal Artillery; Author of 'From Sedan to Saarbrück,' Editor of 'Incidents in the Sepoy War,' &c. With Engravings. Crown 8vo, 7s. 6d.

LAKEMAN. What I saw in Kaffir-land. By Sir STEPHEN LAKEMAN (MAZHAR PACHA). Post 8vo, 8s. 6d.

LAVERGNE. The Rural Economy of England, Scotland, and Ireland. By LEONCE DE LAVERGNE. Translated from the French. With Notes by a Scottish Farmer. 8vo, 12s.

LEE. Lectures on the History of the Church of Scotland, from the Reformation to the Revolution Settlement. By the late Very Rev. JOHN LEE, D.D., LL.D., Principal of the University of Edinburgh. With Notes and Appendices from the Author's Papers. Edited by the Rev. WILLIAM LEE, D.D. 2 vols. 8vo, 21s.

LEE-HAMILTON. Poems and Transcripts. By EUGENE LEE-HAMILTON. Crown 8vo, 6s.

LEWES. The Physiology of Common Life. By GEORGE H. LEWES, Author of 'Sea-side Studies,' &c. Illustrated with numerous Engravings. 2 vols., 12s.

LOCKHART. Doubles and Quits. By Laurence W. M. LOCK-
HART. With Twelve Illustrations. Third Edition. Crown 8vo, 6s.

—— Fair to See : a Novel. Sixth Edition, crown 8vo, 6s.

—— Mine is Thine : a Novel. Sixth Edition, crown 8vo, 6s.

LORIMER. The Institutes of Law : A Treatise of the Principles
of Jurisprudence as determined by Nature. By JAMES LORIMER, Regius
Professor of Public Law and of the Law of Nature and Nations in the University of Edinburgh. New Edition, revised throughout, and much enlarged.
8vo, 18s.

LYON. History of the Rise and Progress of Freemasonry in Scotland. By DAVID MURRAY LYON, Secretary to the Grand Lodge of Scotland.
In small quarto. Illustrated with numerous Portraits of Eminent Members of
the Craft, and Facsimiles of Ancient Charters and other Curious Documents.
£1, 11s. 6d.

M'COMBIE. Cattle and Cattle-Breeders. By WILLIAM M'COMBIE,
Tillyfour. A New and Cheaper Edition, 2s. 6d., cloth.

MACRAE. A Handbook of Deer-Stalking. By ALEXANDER
MACRAE, late Forester to Lord Henry Bentinck. With Introduction by
HORATIO ROSS, Esq. Fcap. 8vo, with two Photographs from Life. 3s. 6d.

M'CRIE. Works of the Rev. Thomas M'Crie, D.D. Uniform Edition. Four vols. crown 8vo, 24s.

—— Life of John Knox. Containing Illustrations of the His-
tory of the Reformation in Scotland. Crown 8vo, 6s. Another Edition, 3s. 6d.

—— Life of Andrew Melville. Containing Illustrations of the
Ecclesiastical and Literary History of Scotland in the Sixteenth and Seventeenth Centuries. Crown 8vo, 6s.

—— History of the Progress and Suppression of the Reformation in Italy in the Sixteenth Century. Crown 8vo, 4s.

—— History of the Progress and Suppression of the Reformation in Spain in the Sixteenth Century. Crown 8vo, 3s. 6d.

—— Sermons, and Review of the ' Tales of My Landlord.' Crown
8vo, 6s.

—— Lectures on the Book of Esther. Fcap. 8vo, 5s.

M'INTOSH. The Book of the Garden. By CHARLES M'INTOSH,
formerly Curator of the Royal Gardens of his Majesty the King of the Belgians,
and lately of those of his Grace the Duke of Buccleuch, K.G., at Dalkeith Pal-
ace. Two large vols. royal 8vo, embellished with 1350 Engravings. £4, 7s. 6d.
Vol. I. On the Formation of Gardens and Construction of Garden Edifices. 776
pages, and 1073 Engravings, £2, 10s.
Vol. II. Practical Gardening. 868 pages, and 279 Engravings, £1, 17s. 6d.

MACKAY. A Manual of Modern Geography ; Mathematical, Physical, and Political. By the Rev. ALEXANDER MACKAY, LL.D., F.R.G.S. New
and Greatly Improved Edition. Crown 8vo, pp. 688. 7s. 6d.

—— Elements of Modern Geography. 46th Thousand, revised
to the present time. Crown 8vo, pp. 300, 3s.

—— The Intermediate Geography. Intended as an Interme-
diate Book between the Author's ' Outlines of Geography,' and ' Elements of
Geography.' Sixth Edition, crown 8vo, pp. 224, 2s.

—— Outlines of Modern Geography. 131st Thousand, revised to the Present Time. 18mo, pp. 112, 1s.

—— First Steps in Geography. 69th Thousand. 18mo, pp.
56. Sewed, 4d. ; cloth, 6d.

—— Elements of Physiography and Physical Geography.
With Express Reference to the Instructions recently issued by the Science and
Art Department. 15th Thousand. Crown 8vo, 1s. 6d.

MACKAY. Facts and Dates ; or, the Leading Events in Sacred and Profane History, and the Principal Facts in the various Physical Sciences. The Memory being aided throughout by a Simple and Natural Method. For Schools and Private Reference. New Edition, thoroughly Revised. Crown 8vo, 3s. 6d.

MACKENZIE. Studies in Roman Law. With Comparative Views of the Laws of France, England, and Scotland. By LORD MACKENZIE, one of the Judges of the Court of Session in Scotland. Fifth Edition, Edited by JOHN KIRKPATRICK, Esq., M.A. Cantab. ; Dr Jur. Heidelb. ; LL.B., Edin ; Advocate. 8vo, 12s.

MANNERS. Notes of an Irish Tour in 1846. By Lord JOHN MANNERS, M.P., G.C.B. New Edition, crown 8vo. 2s. 6d.

MARMORNE. The Story is told by ADOLPHUS SEGRAVE, the youngest of three Brothers. Third Edition. Crown 8vo, 6s.

MARSHALL. French Home Life. By FREDERIC MARSHALL. CONTENTS : Servants.—Children.—Furniture.—Food.—Manners.—Language.—Dress. —Marriage. Second Edition. 5s.

MARSHMAN. History of India. From the Earliest Period to the Close of the India Company's Government , with an Epitome of Subsequent Events. By JOHN CLARK MARSHMAN, C.S I. Abridged from the Author's larger work. Second Edition, revised. Crown 8vo, with Map, 6s. 6d.

MARTIN. Goethe's Faust. Translated by Sir THEODORE MARTIN, K.C.B. Second Edition, crown 8vo, 6s. Cheap Edition, 3s. 6d.

———— The Works of Horace. Translated into English Verse, with Life and Notes. Fourth Edition. In 2 vols. crown 8vo, printed on hand-made paper. [In the press.

———— Poems and Ballads of Heinrich Heine. Done into English Verse. Printed on papier vergé, crown 8vo, 8s.

———— Catullus. With Life and Notes. Second Edition, post 8vo, 7s. 6d.

———— The Vita Nuova of Dante. With an Introduction and Notes. Second Edition, crown 8vo, 5s.

———— Aladdin : A Dramatic Poem. By ADAM OEHLENSCHLAEGER. Fcap. 8vo, 5s.

———— Correggio : A Tragedy. By OEHLENSCHLAEGER. With Notes. Fcap. 8vo, 3s.

———— King Rene's Daughter : A Danish Lyrical Drama. By HENRIK HERTZ. Second Edition, fcap., 2s. 6d.

MEIKLEJOHN. An Old Educational Reformer—Dr Bell. By J. M. D. MEIKLEJOHN, M.A., Professor of the Theory, History, and Practice of Education in the University of St Andrews. Crown 8vo, 3s. 6d.

MINTO. A Manual of English Prose Literature, Biographical and Critical : designed mainly to show Characteristics of Style. By W. MINTO, M.A., Professor of Logic in the University of Aberdeen. Second Edition, revised. Crown 8vo, 7s. 6d.

———— Characteristics of English Poets, from Chaucer to Shirley. Crown 8vo, 9s.

MITCHELL. Biographies of Eminent Soldiers of the last Four Centuries. By Major-General JOHN MITCHELL, Author of 'Life of Wallenstein.' With a Memoir of the Author. 8vo, 9s.

MOIR. Poetical Works of D. M. MOIR (Delta). With Memoir by THOMAS AIRD, and Portrait. Second Edition, 2 vols. fcap. 8vo, 12s.

———— Domestic Verses. New Edition, fcap. 8vo, cloth gilt, 4s. 6d.

———— Lectures on the Poetical Literature of the Past Half-Century. Third Edition, fcap. 8vo, 5s.

———— Life of Mansie Wauch, Tailor in Dalkeith. With 8 Illustrations on Steel, by the late GEORGE CRUIKSHANK. Crown 8vo. 3s. 6d. Another Edition, fcap. 8vo, 1s. 6d.

MONTAGUE. Campaigning in South Africa. Reminiscences of an Officer in 1879. By Captain W. E. MONTAGUE, 94th Regiment, Author of 'Claude Meadowleigh,' &c. 8vo, 10s. 6d.

MONTALEMBERT. Count de Montalembert's History of the Monks of the West. From St Benedict to St Bernard. Translated by Mrs OLIPHANT. 7 vols. 8vo, £3, 17s. 6d.

———— Memoir of Count de Montalembert. A Chapter of Recent French History. By Mrs OLIPHANT, Author of the 'Life of Edward Irving,' &c. 2 vols. crown 8vo, £1, 4s.

MURDOCH. Manual of the Law of Insolvency and Bankruptcy: Comprehending a Summary of the Law of Insolvency, Notour Bankruptcy, Composition-contracts, Trust-deeds, Cessios, and Sequestrations; and the Winding-up of Joint-Stock Companies in Scotland; with Annotations on the various Insolvency and Bankruptcy Statutes; and with Forms of Procedure applicable to these Subjects. By JAMES MURDOCH, Member of the Faculty of Procurators in Glasgow. Fourth Edition, Revised and Enlarged, 8vo, £1.

NEAVES. A Glance at some of the Principles of Comparative Philology. As illustrated in the Latin and Anglican Forms of Speech. By the Hon. Lord NEAVES. Crown 8vo, 1s. 6d.

———— Songs and Verses, Social and Scientific. By an Old Contributor to 'Maga.' Fifth Edition, fcap. 8vo, 4s.

———— The Greek Anthology. Being Vol. XX. of 'Ancient Classics for English Readers.' Crown 8vo, 2s. 6d.

NEW VIRGINIANS, THE. By the Author of 'Estelle Russell,' 'Junia,' &c. In 2 vols., post 8vo, 18s.

NICHOLSON. A Manual of Zoology, for the Use of Students. With a General Introduction on the Principles of Zoology. By HENRY ALLEYNE NICHOLSON, M.D., F.R.S.E., F.G.S., &c., Professor of Natural History in the University of St Andrews. Sixth Edition, revised and enlarged. Crown 8vo, pp. 866, with 452 Engravings on Wood, 14s.

———— Text-Book of Zoology, for the Use of Schools. Third Edition, enlarged. Crown 8vo, with 225 Engravings on Wood, 6s.

———— Introductory Text-Book of Zoology, for the Use of Junior Classes. Third Edition, revised and enlarged, with 136 Engravings, 3s.

———— Outlines of Natural History, for Beginners; being Descriptions of a Progressive Series of Zoological Types. Second Edition, with Engravings, 1s. 6d.

NICHOLSON. A Manual of Palæontology, for the Use of Students. With a General Introduction on the Principles of Palæontology. Second Edition. Revised and greatly enlarged. 2 vols. 8vo, with 722 Engravings, £2, 2s.

——— The Ancient Life-History of the Earth. An Outline of the Principles and Leading Facts of Palæontological Science. Crown 8vo, with numerous Engravings, 10s. 6d.

——— On the "Tabulate Corals" of the Palæozoic Period, with Critical Descriptions of Illustrative Species. Illustrated with 15 Lithograph Plates and numerous Engravings. Super-royal 8vo, 21s.

——— On the Structure and Affinities of the Genus Monticulipora and its Sub-Genera, with Critical Descriptions of Illustrative Species. Illustrated with numerous Engravings on wood and lithographed Plates. Super-royal 8vo. 18s.

NICHOLSON. Redeeming the Time, and other Sermons. By the late Maxwell Nicholson, D.D., Minister of St Stephen's, Edinburgh. Crown 8vo, 7s. 6d.

——— Communion with Heaven, and other Sermons. Crown 8vo, 5s. 6d.

——— Rest in Jesus. Sixth Edition. Fcap. 8vo, 4s. 6d.

OLIPHANT. The Land of Gilead. With Excursions in the Lebanon. By Laurence Oliphant, Author of 'Lord Elgin's Mission to China and Japan,' &c. With Illustrations and Maps. Demy 8vo, 21s.

——— Piccadilly: A Fragment of Contemporary Biography. With Eight Illustrations by Richard Doyle. Fifth Edition, 4s. 6d. Cheap Edition, in paper cover, 2s. 6d.

——— Russian Shores of the Black Sea in the Autumn of 1852. With a Voyage down the Volga and a Tour through the Country of the Don Cossacks. 8vo, with Map and other Illustrations. Fourth Edition, 14s.

OLIPHANT. Historical Sketches of the Reign of George Second. By Mrs Oliphant. Third Edition, 6s.

——— The Story of Valentine; and his Brother. 5s., cloth.

——— Katie Stewart. 2s. 6d.

——— Salem Chapel. 2s. 6d., cloth.

——— The Perpetual Curate. 2s. 6d., cloth.

——— Miss Marjoribanks. 2s. 6d., cloth.

——— The Rector, and the Doctor's Family. 1s. 6d., cloth.

——— John : A Love Story. 2s. 6d., cloth.

OSBORN. Narratives of Voyage and Adventure. By Admiral Sherard Osborn, C.B. 3 vols. crown 8vo, 12s. Or separately:—

——— Stray Leaves from an Arctic Journal ; or, Eighteen Months in the Polar Regions in Search of Sir John Franklin's Expedition in 1850-51. To which is added the Career, Last Voyage, and Fate of Captain Sir John Franklin. New Edition, crown 8vo, 3s. 6d.

——— The Discovery of a North-West Passage by H.M.S. Investigator, during the years 1850-51-52-53-54. Edited from the Logs and Journals of Captain Robert C. M'Clure. Fourth Edition, crown 8vo, 3s. 6d.

——— Quedah ; A Cruise in Japanese Waters : and, The Fight on the Peiho. New Edition, crown 8vo, 5s.

OSSIAN. The Poems of Ossian in the Original Gaelic. With a Literal Translation into English, and a Dissertation on the Authenticity of the Poems. By the Rev. Archibald Clerk. 2 vols. imperial 8vo, £1, 11s. 6d.

PAGE. Introductory Text-Book of Geology. By DAVID PAGE, LL.D., Professor of Geology in the Durham University of Physical Science, Newcastle. With Engravings on Wood and Glossarial Index. Eleventh Edition, 2s. 6d.

———— Advanced Text-Book of Geology, Descriptive and Industrial. With Engravings, and Glossary of Scientific Terms. Sixth Edition, revised and enlarged, 7s. 6d.

———— Handbook of Geological Terms, Geology, and Physical Geography. Second Edition, enlarged, 7s. 6d.

———— Geology for General Readers. A Series of Popular Sketches in Geology and Palæontology. Third Edition, enlarged, 6s.

———— Chips and Chapters. A Book for Amateurs and Young Geologists. 5s.

———— The Past and Present Life of the Globe. With numerous Illustrations. Crown 8vo, 6s.

———— The Crust of the Earth : A Handy Outline of Geology. Sixth Edition, 1s.

———— Economic Geology ; or, Geology in its relation to the Arts and Manufactures. With Engravings, and Coloured Map of the British Islands. Crown 8vo, 7s. 6d.

———— Introductory Text-Book of Physical Geography. With Sketch-Maps and Illustrations. Ninth Edition, 2s. 6d.

———— Advanced Text-Book of Physical Geography. Second Edition. With Engravings. 5s.

PAGET. Paradoxes and Puzzles : Historical, Judicial, and Literary. Now for the first time published in Collected Form. By JOHN PAGET, Barrister-at-Law. 8vo, 12s.

PATON. Spindrift. By Sir J. NOEL PATON. Fcap., cloth, 5s.

———— Poems by a Painter. Fcap., cloth, 5s.

PATTERSON. Essays in History and Art. By R. H. PATTERSON. 8vo, 12s.

PAUL. History of the Royal Company of Archers, the Queen's Body-Guard for Scotland. By JAMES BALFOUR PAUL, Advocate of the Scottish Bar. Crown 4to, with Portraits and other Illustrations. £2, 2s.

PAUL. Analysis and Critical Interpretation of the Hebrew Text of the Book of Genesis. Preceded by a Hebrew Grammar, and Dissertations on the Genuineness of the Pentateuch, and on the Structure of the Hebrew Language. By the Rev. WILLIAM PAUL, A.M. 8vo, 18s.

PERSONALITY. The Beginning and End of Metaphysics, and the Necessary Assumption in all Positive Philosophy. Crown 8vo, 3s.

By THE SAME.

The Origin of Evil, and Other Sermons. Crown 8vo, 4s. 6d.

PETTIGREW. The Handy Book of Bees, and their Profitable Management. By A. PETTIGREW. Fourth Edition, Enlarged, with Engravings. Crown 8vo, 3s. 6d.

PHILOSOPHICAL CLASSICS **FOR** ENGLISH READERS. Companion Series to Ancient and Foreign Classics for English Readers. Edited by WILLIAM KNIGHT, LL.D., Professor of Moral Philosophy, University of St Andrews. In crown 8vo volumes, with portraits, price 3s. 6d.

1. DESCARTES. By Professor Mahaffy, Dublin.
2. BUTLER. By the Rev. W. Lucas Collins, M.A., Honorary Canon of Peterborough.
3. BERKELEY. By Professor A. Campbell Fraser, Edinburgh.
4. FICHTE. By Professor **Adamson,** Owen's College, Manchester.

POLLOK. The Course of Time : A Poem. By ROBERT POLLOK, A.M. Small fcap. 8vo, cloth gilt, 2s. 6d. The Cottage Edition, 32mo, sewed, 8d. The Same, cloth, gilt edges, 1s. 6d. Another Edition, with Illustrations by Birket Foster and others, fcap., gilt cloth, **3s.** 6d., or with **edges** gilt, 4s.

PORT ROYAL **LOGIC.** Translated from the French : with Introduction, Notes, and Appendix. By THOMAS SPENCER BAYNES, **LL.D.,** Professor in the University of St Andrews. Eighth Edition, 12mo, **4s.**

POTTS AND DARNELL. Aditus Faciliores : An easy Latin **Construing** Book, with Complete Vocabulary. By A. W. POTTS, M.A., LL.D., Head-Master of the Fettes College, Edinburgh, and sometime Fellow of St John's College, Cambridge ; and the Rev. C. DARNELL, M.A., Head-Master of Cargilfield Preparatory School, Edinburgh, and late Scholar of Pembroke and Downing Colleges, Cambridge. Sixth Edition, fcap. 8vo, 3s. 6d.

———— **Aditus** Faciliores Graeci. An easy Greek Construing Book, with Complete Vocabulary. Third Edition, fcap. **8vo, 3s.**

PRINGLE. The Live-Stock **of the Farm.** By ROBERT O. PRINGLE. **Third Edition,** crown 8vo. [*In the press.*

PUBLIC GENERAL STATUTES AFFECTING SCOTLAND, **from** 1707 to 1847, with Chronological Table and Index. 3 vols. large 8vo, £3, 3s.

PUBLIC GENERAL STATUTES AFFECTING **SCOTLAND,** COLLECTION OF. Published Annually with General Index.

RAMSAY. Two Lectures on the Genius of Handel, and the Distinctive Character of his Sacred Compositions. Delivered to the Members **of** the Edinburgh Philosophical Institution. By the Very Rev. DEAN RAMSAY, Author of 'Reminiscences of Scottish Life and Character.' Crown 8vo, 3s. 6d.

RANKINE. A Treatise **on** the Rights and Burdens Incident **to** the Ownership of Lands **and** other Heritages in Scotland. By JOHN RANKINE, M.A., Advocate. Large 8vo, 40s.

READE. A Woman-Hater. By CHARLES READE. 3 **vols. crown** 8vo, £1, 5s. 6d. Originally published in 'Blackwood's Magazine.'

REID. A Handy Manual of **German** Literature. By M. **F. REID.** For Schools, Civil Service **Competitions,** and University Local Examinations. Fcap. 8vo, **3s.**

ROBERTSON. Orellana, and other Poems. **By J.** LOGIE ROBERTSON. Fcap. 8vo. **Printed** on hand-made paper. [*In the press.*

RUSTOW. The War for the Rhine Frontier, 1870 : Its Political **and** Military History. By Col. W. RUSTOW. Translated from the German, **by JOHN** LAYLAND NEEDHAM, Lieutenant R.M. Artillery. 3 vols. 8vo, with **Maps and** Plans, £1, 11s. 6d.

ST STEPHENS ; or, Illustrations **of** Parliamentary Oratory. A Poem. *Comprising*—Pym—Vane—Strafford—Halifax—Shaftesbury—St John —Sir R. Walpole—Chesterfield—Carteret—Chatham—Pitt—Fox—Burke— Sheridan — Wilberforce — Wyndham — Conway — Castlereagh — William Lamb (Lord Melbourne)—Tierney—Lord Gray—O'Connell—Plunkett—Shiel—Follett —Macaulay—Peel. Second Edition, crown **8vo, 5s.**

SANDFORD AND TOWNSEND. The Great Governing Families of England. By J. LANGTON SANDFORD and MEREDITH TOWNSEND. 2 vols. 8vo, 15s., in extra binding, with richly-gilt cover.

SCHETKY. Ninety Years of Work and Play. Sketches from the Public and Private Career of JOHN CHRISTIAN SCHETKY, late Marine Painter in Ordinary to the Queen. By his DAUGHTER. Crown 8vo, 7s. 6d.

SCOTTISH NATURALIST, THE. A Quarterly Magazine of Natural History. Edited by F. BUCHANAN WHITE, M.D., F.L.S. Annual Subscription, free by post, 4s.

SELLAR. Manual of the Education Acts for Scotland. By ALEXANDER CRAIG SELLAR, Advocate. Seventh Edition, greatly enlarged, and revised to the present time. 8vo, 15s.

SELLER AND STEPHENS. Physiology at the Farm; in Aid of Rearing and Feeding the Live Stock. By WILLIAM SELLER, M.D., F.R.S.E., Fellow of the Royal College of Physicians, Edinburgh, formerly Lecturer on Materia Medica and Dietetics; and HENRY STEPHENS, F.R.S.E., Author of 'The Book of the Farm,' &c. Post 8vo, with Engravings, 16s.

SETON. St Kilda: Past and Present. By GEORGE SETON, M.A. Oxon.; Author of the 'Law and Practice of Heraldry in Scotland,' &c. With appropriate Illustrations. Small quarto, 15s.

SHADWELL. The Life of Colin Campbell, Lord Clyde. Illustrated by Extracts from his Diary and Correspondence. By Lieutenant-General SHADWELL, C.B. 2 vols. 8vo. With Portrait, Maps, and Plans. 36s.

SIMPSON. Paris after Waterloo: A Revised Edition of a "Visit to Flanders and the Field of Waterloo." By JAMES SIMPSON, Advocate. With 2 coloured Plans of the Battle. Crown 8vo, 5s.

SMITH. Italian Irrigation: A Report on the Agricultural Canals of Piedmont and Lombardy, addressed to the Hon. the Directors of the East India Company; with an Appendix, containing a Sketch of the Irrigation System of Northern and Central India. By Lieut.-Col. R. BAIRD SMITH, F.G.S., Captain, Bengal Engineers. Second Edition. 2 vols. 8vo, with Atlas in folio, 30s.

SMITH. Thorndale; or, The Conflict of Opinions. By WILLIAM SMITH, Author of 'A Discourse on Ethics,' &c. A New Edition. Crown 8vo, 10s. 6d.

——— Gravenhurst; or, Thoughts on Good and Evil. Second Edition, with Memoir of the Author. Crown 8vo, 8s.

——— A Discourse on Ethics of the School of Paley. 8vo, 4s.

——— Dramas. 1. Sir William Crichton. 2. Athelwold. 3. Guidone. 24mo, boards, 3s.

SOUTHEY. Poetical Works of Caroline Bowles Southey. Fcap. 8vo, 5s.

——— The Birthday, and other Poems. Second Edition, 5s.

——— Chapters on Churchyards. Fcap., 2s. 6d.

SPEKE. What led to the Discovery of the Nile Source. By JOHN HANNING SPEKE, Captain H.M. Indian Army. 8vo, with Maps, &c., 14s.

——— Journal of the Discovery of the Source of the Nile. By J. H. SPEKE, Captain H.M. Indian Army. With a Map of Eastern Equatorial Africa by Captain SPEKE; numerous illustrations, chiefly from Drawings by Captain GRANT; and Portraits, engraved on Steel, of Captains SPEKE and GRANT. 8vo, 21s.

STARFORTH. Villa Residences and Farm Architecture : A Series of Designs. By JOHN STARFORTH, Architect. 102 Engravings. Second Edition, medium 4to, £2, 17s. 6d.

STATISTICAL ACCOUNT OF SCOTLAND. Complete, with Index, 15 vols. 8vo, £16, 16s.

Each County sold separately, with Title, Index, and Map, **neatly bound in cloth,** forming a very valuable Manual to the Landowner, the **Tenant, the Manufacturer,** the Naturalist, the Tourist, **&c.**

STEPHENS. The **Book** of the Farm ; detailing the **Labours of the** Farmer, Farm-Steward, Ploughman, Shepherd, Hedger, Farm-Labourer, **Field-**Worker, and Cattleman. By HENRY STEPHENS, F.R.S.E. Illustrated **with** Portraits of Animals painted from the life ; and with 557 Engravings on **Wood,** representing the principal Field Operations, Implements, and **Animals treated** of in the Work. A New and Revised Edition, the third, in **great part Re-**written. 2 vols. large 8vo, £2, 10s.

———— The **Book** of Farm-Buildings ; their Arrangement **and** Construction. By HENRY STEPHENS, F.R.S.E., Author of 'The Book of the Farm ,' and ROBERT SCOTT BURN. Illustrated with 1045 Plates and Engravings. Large 8vo, uniform with 'The Book of the Farm,' &c. £1, 11s. 6d.

———— The Book of Farm Implements **and Machines. By J.** SLIGHT and R. SCOTT BURN, Engineers. Edited **by HENRY STEPHENS.** Large 8vo, uniform with 'The Book of the Farm,' £2, 2s.

———— Catechism of Practical Agriculture. With Engravings. 1s.

STEWART. Advice to Purchasers of Horses. By JOHN STEWART, **V.S.** Author of 'Stable Economy.' 2s. 6d.

———— Stable Economy. A Treatise on the Management of Horses in relation to Stabling, **Grooming, Feeding, Watering,** and Working. Seventh Edition, fcap. 8vo, 6s. 6d.

STIRLING. Missing Proofs : a Pembrokeshire Tale. By M. C. STIRLING, Author of 'The Grahams of Invermoy.' 2 vols. crown 8vo.

[In the press.

STORMONTH. Etymological and Pronouncing Dictionary of the English Language. Including a very Copious Selection of Scientific **Terms.** For Use in Schools and Colleges, and as a Book of General Reference. **By the** Rev. JAMES STORMONTH. The Pronunciation carefully Revised by the **Rev.** P. H. PHELP, M.A. Cantab. Sixth Edition, with enlarged Supplement, containing many words not to be found in any other Dictionary. Crown **8vo,** pp. 800. 7s. 6d.

———— The School Etymological Dictionary **and Word-Book.** Combining the advantages of an ordinary pronouncing School **Dictionary and** an Etymological Spelling-book. Fcap. 8vo, pp. 254. 2s

STORY. Graffiti D'Italia. By W. W. STORY, Author of 'Roba di Roma.' Second Edition, fcap. 8vo, 7s. 6d.

———— Nero ; **A** Historical **Play.** Fcap. 8vo, 6s.

———— Vallombrosa. **Post 8vo.**

STRICKLAND. Lives of the Queens of Scotland, and English Princesses connected with the Regal Succession of Great Britain. By AGNES STRICKLAND. With Portraits and Historical Vignettes. 8 vols. post 8vo, £4, 4s.

STURGIS. John - a - Dreams. A Tale. By JULIAN STURGIS. New Edition, crown 8vo, 3s. 6d.

———— An Accomplished Gentleman. Second Edition. Post 8vo, 7s. 6d.

SUTHERLAND. Handbook of Hardy Herbaceous and Alpine Flowers, for general Garden Decoration. Containing Descriptions, in Plain Language, of upwards of 1000 Species of Ornamental Hardy Perennial and Alpine Plants, adapted to all classes of Flower-Gardens, Rockwork, and Waters; along with Concise and Plain Instructions for their Propagation and Culture. By WILLIAM SUTHERLAND, Gardener to the Earl of Minto; formerly Manager of the Herbaceous Department at Kew. Crown 8vo, 7s. 6d.

SWAINSON. A Handbook of Weather Folk-Lore. Being a Collection of Proverbial Sayings in various Languages relating to the Weather, with Explanatory and Illustrative Notes. By the Rev. C. SWAINSON, M.A., Vicar of High Hurst Wood. Fcap. 8vo, Roxburghe binding, 6s. 6d.

SWAYNE. Lake Victoria: A Narrative of Explorations in Search of the Source of the Nile. Compiled from the Memoirs of Captains Speke and Grant. By GEORGE C. SWAYNE, M.A., late Fellow of Corpus Christi College, Oxford. Illustrated with Woodcuts and Map. Crown 8vo, 7s. 6d.

TAYLOR. Destruction and Reconstruction: Personal Experiences of the Late War in the United States. By RICHARD TAYLOR, Lieutenant-General in the Confederate Army. 8vo, 10s. 6d.

TAYLOR. The Story of My Life. By the late Colonel MEADOWS TAYLOR, Author of 'The Confessions of a Thug,' &c. &c. Edited by his Daughter. Third Edition, post 8vo, 9s.

THOLUCK. Hours of Christian Devotion. Translated from the German of A. Tholuck, D.D., Professor of Theology in the University of Halle. By the Rev ROBERT MENZIES, D.D. With a Preface written for this Translation by the Author. Second Edition, crown 8vo, 7s. 6d.

THOMSON. Handy Book of the Flower-Garden: being Practical Directions for the Propagation, Culture, and Arrangement of Plants in Flower-Gardens all the year round. Embracing all classes of Gardens, from the largest to the smallest. With Engraved and Coloured Plans, illustrative of the various systems of Grouping in Beds and Borders. By DAVID THOMSON, Gardener to his Grace the Duke of Buccleuch, K.G., at Drumlanrig. Third Edition, crown 8vo, 7s. 6d.

——— The Handy Book of Fruit-Culture under Glass: being a series of Elaborate Practical Treatises on the Cultivation and Forcing of Pines, Vines, Peaches, Figs, Melons, Strawberries, and Cucumbers. With Engravings of Hothouses, &c., most suitable for the Cultivation and Forcing of these Fruits. Crown 8vo, with Engravings, 7s. 6d.

THOMSON. A Practical Treatise on the Cultivation of the Grape-Vine. By WILLIAM THOMSON, Tweed Vineyards. Ninth Edition, 8vo, 5s.

TOM CRINGLE'S LOG. A New Edition, with Illustrations. Crown 8vo, cloth gilt, 5s. Cheap Edition, 2s.

TRANSACTIONS OF THE HIGHLAND AND AGRICULTURAL SOCIETY OF SCOTLAND. Published annually, price 5s.

TULLOCH. Rational Theology and Christian Philosophy in England in the Seventeenth Century. By JOHN TULLOCH, D.D., Principal of St Mary's College in the University of St Andrews; and one of her Majesty's Chaplains in Ordinary in Scotland. Second Edition. 2 vols. 8vo, 28s.

——— Some Facts of Religion and of Life. Sermons Preached before her Majesty the Queen in Scotland, 1866-76. Second Edition, crown 8vo, 7s. 6d.

TULLOCH. **The** Christian Doctrine of Sin ; being the Croall Lecture for 1876. Crown 8vo, 6s.

———— **Theism.** The Witness of Reason **and Nature to an All-**Wise and Beneficent Creator. 8vo, 10s. 6d.

TYTLER. **The** Wonder-Seeker; or, **The** History of Charles Douglas. By M. FRASER TYTLER, Author of 'Tales of the Great and Brave,' &c. A New Edition. Fcap., 3s. 6d.

VIRGIL. The Æneid of Virgil. **Translated in** English **Blank** Verse by G. **K. RICKARDS, M.A., and Lord RAVENSWORTH.** 2 vols. fcap. 8vo, 10s.

WALFORD. Mr Smith : **A** Part of his Life. **By L. B. WALFORD.** Cheap Edition, 3s. 6d.

———— **Pauline.** Fifth Edition. Crown 8vo, 6s.

———— **Cousins. Cheaper** Edition. **Crown** 8vo, 6s.

———— Troublesome Daughters. Cheaper Edition. **Crown 8vo, 6s.**

WARREN'S (SAMUEL) WORKS. People's Edition, **4 vols.** crown 8vo, cloth, 18s. Or separately :—

Diary of a Late Physician. **3s. 6d. Illustrated, crown 8vo, 7s. 6d.**

Ten Thousand A-Year. **5s.**

Now and Then. The Lily and the Bee. **Intellectual and** Moral Development of the Present Age. 4s. 6d.

Essays : **Critical, Imaginative, and Juridical. 5s.**

WARREN. The Five Books **of** the Psalms. With Marginal Notes. By Rev. SAMUEL L. WARREN, Rector of Esher, Surrey ; late Fellow, Dean, and Divinity Lecturer, Wadham College, Oxford. Crown 8vo, 5s.

WELLINGTON. Wellington Prize Essays on **"the System of Field** Manœuvres best adapted for enabling our Troops **to meet a Continental Army."** Edited by Sir EDWARD BRUCE HAMLEY, C.B. **8vo, 12s. 6d.**

WESTMINSTER ASSEMBLY. Minutes **of the W**estminster As-sembly, while engaged in preparing their Directory for Church Government, Confession of Faith, and Catechisms (November 1644 to March 1649). Printed from Transcripts of the Originals procured by the General Assembly of the Church of Scotland. Edited by the Rev. ALEX. T. MITCHELL, D.D., Professor of Ecclesiastical History in the University of St Andrews, and the Rev. JOHN STRUTHERS, LL.D., Minister of Prestonpans. With a Historical and Critical Introduction by Professor Mitchell. 8vo, 15s.

WHITE. **The Eighteen Christian Centuries. By the Rev. JAMES** WHITE, Author of 'The History of France.' Seventh Edition, post 8vo, with Index, 6s.

———— History of France, **from the Earliest Times. Sixth Thou-**sand, post 8vo, with Index, 6s.

WHITE. Archæological Sketches in Scotland—Kintyre and Knapdale. By Captain T. P. WHITE, R.E., of the Ordnance Survey. With numerous Illustrations. 2 vols. folio, £4, 4s. Vol. I., Kintyre, sold separately, £2, 2s.

WILLS AND **GREENE.** Drawing-room Dramas for Children. By W. G. WILLS and the Hon. Mrs GREENE. Crown 8vo, 6s.

WILSON. The "Ever-Victorious Army:" A History of the Chinese Campaign under Lieut.-Col. C. G. Gordon, and of the Suppression of the Tai-ping Rebellion. By ANDREW WILSON, F.A.S.L. 8vo, with Maps, 15s.

—— The Abode of Snow: Observations on a Journey from Chinese Tibet to the Indian Caucasus, through the Upper Valleys of the Himalaya. New Edition. Crown 8vo, with Map, 10s. 6d.

WILSON. Works of Professor Wilson. Edited by his Son-in-Law, Professor FERRIER. 12 vols. crown 8vo, £2, 8s.

—— Christopher in his Sporting-Jacket. 2 vols., 8s.

—— Isle of Palms, City of the Plague, and other Poems. 4s.

—— Lights and Shadows of Scottish Life, and other Tales. 4s.

—— Essays, Critical and Imaginative. 4 vols., 16s.

—— The Noctes Ambrosianæ. Complete, 4 vols., 14s.

—— The Comedy of the Noctes Ambrosianæ. By CHRISTOPHER NORTH. Edited by JOHN SKELTON, Advocate. With a Portrait of Professor Wilson and of the Ettrick Shepherd, engraved on Steel. Crown 8vo, 7s. 6d.

—— Homer and his Translators, and the Greek Drama. Crown 8vo, 4s.

WINGATE. Annie Weir, and other Poems. By DAVID WINGATE. Fcap. 8vo, 5s.

—— Lily Neil. A Poem. Crown 8vo, 4s. 6d.

WORSLEY. Poems and Translations. By PHILIP STANHOPE WORSLEY, M.A. Edited by EDWARD WORSLEY. Second Edition, enlarged. Fcap. 8vo, 6s.

WYLDE. A Dreamer. By KATHARINE WYLDE. In 3 vols., post 8vo, 25s. 6d.

YOUNG. Songs of Béranger done into English Verse. By WILLIAM YOUNG. New Edition, revised. Fcap. 8vo, 4s. 6d.

YULE. Fortification: for the Use of Officers in the Army, and Readers of Military History. By Col. YULE, Bengal Engineers. 8vo, with numerous Illustrations, 10s. 6d.

www.ingramcontent.com/pod-product-compliance
Lightning Source LLC
Chambersburg PA
CBHW032007010726
47493CB00007B/2312